# RAGIN'
# CAJUN

## GEORGE ONSTOT

ISBN: 0988157187
ISBN-13: 978-0-9881571-8-7

THIS IS FOR J.C.O.

# CONTENTS

Chapter 1     9

Chapter 2     45

Chapter 3     73

Chapter 4     107

Chapter 5     135

Chapter 6     155

Chapter 7     187

Chapter 8     211

Chapter 9     233

Chapter 10    259

Chapter 11    285

Chapter 12    305

ALSO BY GEORGE ONSTOT

*Bullies on Juice*
*Macho Fellows*
*What's Your Problem?*
*Entrepreneur*
*Bum Love*

# CHAPTER 1

"San Francisco is unique, maybe the most exhilarating city in America," said Desirée Dupree. Above her, a sign saying ON THE AIR glowed red. "This is the town folks dream about. I mean, who leaves his heart in Denver? The city's location, views, cultural and political sophistication, lifestyle, beauty, weather, topography and history...it's 'everybody's favorite city.' If not to live in, at least to visit.

"San Francisco is regularly voted by various magazines as the world's most popular tourist destination. The city's aberrations, idiosyncrasies and cutting-edge social policies are legendary, often the subject of front-page national-news stories: legitimizing domestic-partnership agreements. Limiting highrise development. Enacting God knows how many official boycotts and making other municipal foreign-policy forays. Instituting the country's toughest pesticide ban. Setting safety standards for video display terminals. Permitting cannabis buyers' clubs for medicinal marijuana use. Banning workplace drug tests. Prohibiting pizza delivery guys from redlining neighborhoods. Placing far-out propositions on city ballots, such as whether a ventriloquist/police officer can take his dummy on his beat. Extending health insurance to cover sex-change operations for municipal employees. Appointing a tranny to the Human Rights Commission. And, perhaps most important, agreeing that the Doggie Diner will, for five years, keep in place a truly disgusting seven-foot-tall dachshund head, topped with a chef's cap, until it becomes City property."

Desirée blew a stream of smoke and stubbed out her tenth Pall Mall. She loved radio. Most of the time, it seemed to love her back. She especially loved KCA's spacious broadcast booth, a vision of gleaming browns and tans with a floor-to-ceiling tinted window that presented a spectacular view of the San Francisco Bay.

Tom from Alameda wanted to talk politics.

"If *I* were president," Desirée said, "I would run as an independent and be my own vice-president. I would mobilize middle-class America. It would be the most challenging fight of my career.

"People are the same whether they're living in barrios, ghettos or reservations, and the 'burbs are really just fancy ghettos. So I believe that any significant action for social change will have to focus on the white middle class for the simple reason that they have most of the power. Our population is still mostly middle class through earning power or value identification. Take the lower-lower middle class, the blue-collar group that's still around if all their jobs haven't yet been exported to China."

Hers was the humblest resumé of any top-rated talk-show host. The week after graduating from New Orleans' LaFleur High School, she had gotten her first radio job as a "rock jock" at the Big Easy's lowest-rated station. Back then, she'd stayed up all night playing dance music for guys who called up to ask what she was wearing. College had been as unaffordable as a Mercedes. She liked to joke that she had a high school diploma and a Ph.D. in common sense—"no B.A., no B.S." Her campus had been the public library, where she scrutinized *Time, Newsweek, U.S. News and World Report,* the daily newspapers. Desirée learned about people, politics, power, prestige and profits. She rarely met an argument she didn't like.

After tuning in to the stars of talk radio—Larry King, Rush Limbaugh, Don Imus and Tom Leykis—she resolved to become one, too. But first she needed to sound less like the Dixie chick she was. An accent was no asset. She started listening to dialect tapes from the library. Neutralizing her Louisiana twang turned out to be easy; she could soon fake an accent as adeptly as any Actors' Studio graduate and soon learned to sound generically American.

From New Orleans she had leapfrogged to Chicago, then Boston, before KCA program director

Kelvin Barrow made her an offer she considered entirely too generous. Next stop, San Francisco.

"Look," she continued to Tom in Alameda, "if, as both president and vice-president, I could manage to organize all the exploited, low-income groups—blacks, Chicanos, Puerto Ricans, poor whites—and then somehow weld them together into a viable coalition that could march down the street and chant, 'We're mad as hell and we're not gonna take it anymore.' People would have to start paying attention. Really, the only hope for the genuine minority progress is to find allies within the majority and organize that great mass of people who are the middle class."

"Do you really think that would go over in America? We're inherently conservative—"

"Like hell. Right now we're nothing. Zero. There are three hundred million of us now and you know what we're doing? 'Lives of quiet desperation,' that's what we've got. Know who said that? Henry David Thoreau, a couple of hundred years ago. He's our most astute social critic today. We're drowning in apathy. We've pursued the American Dream, but it's turned into a nightmare. We're trapped in pointless marriages or escaping into expensive, guilty divorces. We have homes in the suburbs and a car or two but they provide little comfort. Our personal and professional lives are unfulfilling and often frustrating as hell. When it all gets to be too much, we run off to the psychiatrist looking for a quick cure. All he can do is listen to us complain and dope us up with Prozac, Valium or Viagra. We feel alienated and disenfranchised, unable to participate in the political process and fearful that things will never improve. Our utopia has turned into an overpriced condo in a silly suburb and our optimism has turned into disillusionment."

"Speak for yourself, Desirée," said the caller.

"Damn straight...and for you too. And everyone who is listening. We are among the first generations to live in a mass-media-oriented society. Every night we vegetate in front of the TV set and watch the news. Do you know what we see? We see the outrageous hypocrisy and corruption of our national leaders. We see our institutions crumble and our values mocked. Our nation at some point stopped being ours; we start to feel that our individual failures are just part of a much larger failure. I see despair all around me. America right now would be more receptive than ever to such an organizer. I would rub people's noses in it, make them totally aware of why they feel so awful."

"Wouldn't everyone be suspicious of your motives?"

"Yeah, sure. But so what? I would galvanize you for radical social change. I would show you a way to participate in the democratic process, which you obviously have forgotten you have. You could then retaliate against the establishment that oppresses you. You could overcome your apathy. Taxes? Jobs? Consumer problems? Pollution? We could take on all these issues. Then on to the big offenders: Congress and the megacorporations. The effect would snowball. In the end we would reach the real goal: people power. The arrogant bastards on Capitol Hill and in the boardrooms would know who the bosses really were."

"That sounds like so much pie in the sky," said the caller.

She glanced at Jay Otari, her engineer, through the window that separated them. Although Desirée was proficient in using the knobs and switches of radio, at KCA all she had to do was talk.

"We're at the top of the hour. Time for a break. This is Desirée Dupree, the Ragin' Cajun, on KCA, Newstalk Nine-eighty."

She smiled, taking off her headphones. Break time. Each hour on KCA consisted of 44 minutes of programming and 16 minutes of commercials. Then newsbreaks and weather reports. It was no great secret that KCA had the highest advertising rates in town, thanks partly to Desirée Dupree. As she—and her bosses—saw it, her real job was to give her listeners enough of herself in those 44 minutes to make it worthwhile for them to sit through those 16 minutes' worth of commercials.

The slickly produced 30-second spots would continue for the next several minutes, then she would come on for another thirty seconds to remind her listeners to stay tuned. Then the news and more messages form their sponsors.

Only she and Jay were on the premises tonight, unless their intern was still around, which was quite likely; the college boy hated to leave Broadcast House, a shiny brown Rubik's Cube near San Francisco Bay. Desirée loved it too. The lights were dim and the place quiet. Perfect.

At KCA, she brought up the day's most controversial issues, took on all callers and picked apart their arguments as astutely as any trial lawyer. Fortunately, Bay Area radio listeners seemed largely uninterested in her personal life, but when the occasional questions came up, she danced around them; some people, seeing her swarthy face, big white teeth and piercing hazel eyes on the station's Website, guessed once or twice that she was married to some hotshot lawyer and the two sat up in bed most nights, postcoitally debating issues while munching on takeout Chinese food. In reality, she was a woman too busy for sex and chow mein, a workaholic who spent endless hours researching topics and had put her libido on hold indefinitely. She was, more often than not, too busy for makeup and nail polish, though her sister, Monique, kept after her to keep her wavy blonde hair cut into a fashionable shag. Monique also made sure she had Gap khakis, blouses and skirts to wear. It wouldn't do for the queen bee of Bay Area talk radio, although unseen by her audience, to walk around like a Sally Ann poster girl.

Desirée hadn't found her job at KCA; Kelvin Barrow had found *her*. As he explained it to her, Blaine Davison, his early-evening host, a former lawyer whose smooth, man-about-town persona helped make KCA the top station in Arbitron's Bay Area ratings book, learned one morning that his many investments had gone bad and he faced many questions from the Internal Revenue Service. After the search-and-recovery team fished Davison's bloated blue body out of the Bay, Kelvin used fill-in

18

hosts while searching for a permanent replacement. He listened to the myriad unsolicited demo tapes he received weekly and concluded that they all sounded boring as hell.

San Francisco's most popular station needed someone different. Someone who could shake things up.

Through Internet streaming, he discovered Desirée Dupree, three thousand miles away in Boston at WBRS. A young woman, maybe in her early thirties. A smooth, sultry voice, with just the tiniest traces of a Southern accent. Some of KCA's newsreaders were women, but its only female host was a weekend fitness guru. The demographics indicated that the full-time addition of a woman might not be such a bad thing. Kelvin emailed Desirée and introduced himself. He asked her: Are you happy in Beantown?

San Francisco, he told her on the phone, had a reputation as being open and friendly, a mecca for bohemians and homosexuals. He found it closed and snobbish, provincial, filled with moneyed families who had little use for the rest of humankind.

Desirée Dupree, an anarcho-capitalist libertarian on the air in upright, uptight San Francisco? It could make for some damned lively radio. If they don't like you, he said, they will tune in to hate you.

They can hate me all they want, said Desirée Dupree with a laugh. Just so long as they don't ignore me. I'm putting my kid sister through college. I'm in debt up to here.

He offered her the six-till-nine shift, when more people were listening. Desirée wanted the nine-till-midnight shift. She simply felt energized later at night and liked the diverse people who called in. Kelvin consented and offered her more money than she had ever made. She quit her Boston job and flew out with Monique to the City by the Bay. That was two years earlier—both a long time ago and only yesterday.

Desirée lit a cigarette and sat back. The night had

gone well. The next hour would, too, probably. She reminded herself every night that she had a good gig. She also reminded herself that she could lose her good gig if her ratings slipped through no apparent fault of her own.

The ON THE AIR sign flashed above her and she leaned into the microphone to tell her listeners what they already knew. "Stay tuned for Manny Ramirez at midnight, who'll take you through to breakfast here on Newstalk Nine-eighty."

The commercials played on. Desirée took off her headset. Matt McDonald, their intern, knocked on the door. A junior at San Francisco State University, he still felt amazed that he had been accepted into his school's ferociously competitive broadcasting program and had gotten an internship at KCA.

She waved him in. "Matt, what's goin' on? How's the college man?"

"I made the dean's list again." He grinned, as if soon he would be sitting in Desirée's chair. Preferably with her on his lap.

"Up here," she said, offering him a high five. "Say, is this fog supposed to hang around till tomorrow?"

"Not so bad later."

"Good." Desirée worried about Monique. "I hate driving through that shit."

"You get used to it."

"Really?"

Matt smiled. "No."

She smiled back, far too preoccupied to see the love in his eyes. Matt considered her just too fascinating: a smart, sexy gal, powerful and assertive, talented as all hell. How could he be happy with a college girlfriend, which he didn't have, when a *woman* like Desirée existed? Like so many other career-driven women, she was unattached. If she had a boyfriend, Matt would have already met him.

He often indulged in fantasies of evenings with her: dinner and dancing, then home to her place for hot sex and hours of cuddling. But of course, he knew it would never happen. She treated him with the same polite indifference he had gotten from many other desirable women. Desirée Dupree would want a *man,* not some bushy-haired college boy like Matt McDonald. So he kept his feelings to himself and tried to be content with the belief that he and she were friends.

And what did Desirée truly think of Matt? She kept forgetting he was there. Had she paid enough attention to him to discern his feelings, she would have taken his attraction to her as nothing more than the most superficial of compliments. She liked Matt's efficiency and politeness; at work, he *worked*—he didn't just *schmooze* or brownnose with these broadcasters he so clearly admired.

Jay signaled to Desirée that the break was about to end. Matt slinked out the door, and Desirée went back on the air in her big warm room where she held court five nights a week. Sometimes she liked to put on the cordless headset and microphone and wander around the spacious studio as she took calls. She inevitably ended up standing at the huge tinted window, gazing out at nothing in particular, doing some of her most lucid thinking and most eloquent speaking.

"I want to talk about people who have jumped off the Golden Gate Bridge," said Colleen from Berkeley. "Over a thousand people have jumped. Only a couple of dozen have survived, and that was because each of them hit the water feet first. Don't you think it was a good idea to stop allowing pedestrians to walk on the bridge at night?"

"If you prevent people from jumping by closing the bridge to pedestrians," Desirée replied, "they'll just find other ways to end their lives. Anyway, I think the authorities care mainly about just making sure the tourists from Ohio or Oslo don't see someone jumping on a beautiful summer's day or that a jumper just happens to does his final thing while a photographer snaps a postcard photo. A tragic waste of film."

The caller laughed nervously at Desirée's brazenness. No listener would ever guess that the Ragin' Cajun had ever felt a moment of insecurity or uncertainty.

"Jack in San Francisco. This is Desirée Dupree on KCA."

"*Desirée Dupree.*" He fairly hissed the words.

Desirée frowned. "That's me. So, what's on your mind?"

"*You know what I want to talk about.*"

The man's cold and sinister voice made her shoot the quickest glance at Jay, who pumped a fist at her. *Just kick his butt.* She knew how to exploit antagonistic callers.

"Well, dude, it's your dime. Name the topic."

"You whore. You know what you did. You must die—"

"Thank you very much." Desirée hung up and went to the next caller. The trick was to retort with a levity she scarcely felt. KCA had chosen not to have a seven-second delay, so there was no chance to bleep out what callers said. Even if he was some Jeffrey Dahmer-ish prison escapee, he could not gain personal access to her. Broadcast House could have been called Fort Knox by the Bay. Still, troublesome callers unnerved her.

She struggled through the rest of her shift, anxious for midnight. It was uncommon for some weirdo to begin harassing her, but when it happened, she feared, deep down inside, that he might be the one who would not go away.

Minutes after finishing her shift, Desirée took the elevator down to Broadcast House's parkade, climbed into her BMW and crept down Market Street, struggling through a pall of San Francisco fog as thick as clay. She had the radio and heater on but still shivered. Although the drive home was relatively long, the traffic was almost nonexistent. Her big old house was a wonderful refuge from the craziness of downtown San Francisco and KCA.

Her iPhone rang and she smiled as she touched its glowing screen. Monique. "Brat! How come you're still up?"

Desirée knew she should pull off to the side of the

street. She had often chastised her listeners about the dangers of driving while yakking away on a cell phone, and she considered herself no hypocrite. But she also considered herself no idiot, and sitting in a stationary BMW on Market Street talking on the phone after midnight would have been supremely idiotic. She kept driving.

"Dez, I couldn't sleep after I heard that creep on the air." Monique was her sister, best friend and roommate, in that order.

"That's just like you, getting upset over some loser out there who has nothing better to do than bug a talk-show host."

"He sounded like he meant business. Dez, shouldn't you call the cops about this?"

"The cops wouldn't do jackshit."

"Maybe not. But still—"

"They'd just tell me not to get my panties in a bunch."

"Maybe he's just getting started."

Desirée sighed. Monique had a point. "Well, it was just one call from one jerk-off. We have zillions of listeners competing for a dozen lines to rag on me each night. Maybe he'll never get through again." She paused, with one hand on the steering wheel and the other on her phone, thinking how shitty it was that her home, with her nice big bed, still lay several miles away out there somewhere in that damned fog. "Anyway, we'll talk about it later. Promise me you'll be in bed when I get home?"

"You win again," Monique conceded, hanging up. Nearly half an hour later, Desirée finally sat parked in her garage. Getting out of her car, she felt like anything but a winner.

. . .

The man sat in his Tenderloin apartment with the shades drawn. He always kept the sunlight out. The darkness of the apartment matched his mood. He kept the TV on all night sometimes, when he couldn't sleep. He liked to watch DVDs like *Taxi Driver* because he could relate to underground men like Travis Bickle. He lit candles and burned incense.

He had souvenirs from all over, even from his tour of duty in Vietnam. His most prized possession was a photo of Michael, the son he had never had, the greatest friend he could have wanted. Michael was dead now, and that Ragin' Cajun bitch had killed him. So now the man would kill *her*. Simple as that.

Or maybe not so simple. He would torture her first, reduce her to nothing but a babbling, begging mass of protoplasm. After he was done with her, the hell he would send her to would seem like heaven. She would thank him for putting her out of her misery. He knew about torture. He knew how to do it. The Marines had taught him well. The bitch had no idea what suffering was, but he would teach her. Oh, yes, he would. He would be happy to do it.

...

Desirée received just one threatening call each night but that was enough; by Friday her nerves were so jangled that she considered calling in sick. Jay's job as her engineer included screening Desirée's callers, but a sad fact in broadcasting was that even the best screeners couldn't tell the troublemakers from the legitimate callers. Each night, at some point, one of them would be the tormentor. She didn't shoot an angry or accusing glance at Jay, she simply cut off the man as quickly as she could and moved on. Jay, knowing it wasn't *his* fault, no longer even offered to apologize for inadvertently letting the harasser through.

Desirée began having trouble sleeping and eating. She went on the air and delivered her nightly three hours. It was her worst week in a decade.

Who was this guy, and why was he so enraged at her? She knew hatred—she'd heard it in the voices of a hundred callers who despised Uncle Sam, Big Business, the local sports teams. Not just frustration or annoyance but real, honest-to-God, fuck-you hatred. And this man hated Desirée Dupree. But why? She could be callous at times, certainly, and so consumed with work that she forgot about everyone and everything else. But she would never deliberately attack anyone, mentally or physically. Why had this man, in a city where she had lived only a couple of years, made it apparently his full-time job to make her life pure hell?

Hearing someone coming down the hall towards her closet-sized office, she instantly sought an escape route. She thought for a moment of smashing the window with her elbow and leaping out. But the fall would be four floors. She decided to take her chances with the person approaching.

The figure got nearer. She got ready to knee the intruder's groin.

"Desirée...?"

"Oh, Kelvin, it's *you*." She let out a huge breath.

Kelvin Barrow, KCA's program director, was blond, fair, handsome and charismatic. He always looked as if he had just stepped off the cover of *GQ* and seemed unfazed by the pressures of his job. "Didn't mean to startle you."

"You have that effect on women in general."

He grinned. "I guess. Why are you here right now? Well, I'm glad you *are*. We need to deal with this caller more."

"I thought we already agreed to ignore him till he went away."

He shook his head. "*I* didn't agree. I won't have some sociopath bullying one of my people like this."

"I can handle it. I can deal with it. We'll just wait it out until he goes away."

Kelvin frowned. "Apparently you keep forgetting that *I am the boss*." He, in fact, had been in radio long enough to know that his hosts, like children, were performers with blown-glass egos. Off the air they were very much the same as they were on: temperamental, argumentative, demanding, talented, charming. Especially Desirée Dupree, who, at the ripe old age of 28, was at the top and dizzy from the view.

"We've got to act on this caller immediately," he said. "It's always best to stop something minor before it becomes something major. And I'm not so sure I would characterize this as 'minor.'"

Desirée's arms felt covered with gooseflesh as she observed just how seriously her boss took this matter. She wanted him to laugh it off, to assure her that it was merely one of the hazards of public life. But no. He was standing in her office, his handsome face dark with concern.

She rested her hands on her thighs. "So now what?"

"He threatened you on the air. That's illegal. I've called the police. They're here right now. They're waiting to meet you."

He motioned for two people to step into the cramped office.

The woman, tall and swarthy, wore an overcoat and a bemused expression. Her hair was shiny as mink and her eyes were large and dark. An intense woman who had seen her share of difficult cases—and this was presumably an easy one, or at least not yet a hard one.

The man with her was quite formidable indeed, half

a head taller, with a mane brown and wavy, his shoulders broad. He wore a sportscoat that needed replacing, a tie, wide and garish, from decades past.

Desirée and he stared at each other. His eyes were the coldest, most indifferent blue, yet somehow penetrating. His mouth was grim, his jawline strong and clean. If his partner looked tough, he looked tougher. Desirée wondered how many murder investigations this relatively young man had conducted. Far too many.

"Mr. Barrow," the woman cop was saying, "we need to get down to business."

"You tricked me, Kelvin," Desirée said. "You called them behind my back."

"Yep." He turned to the cops. "This, as you may have guessed, is Desirée Dupree. The Ragin' Cajun."

"I'm Inspector Christina Anchor," said the woman. "And this is Inspector Harris Cavanaugh."

"Thanks for coming down," said Kelvin.

Desirée's office was far too small for all of them, so she remained seated while the other three stood over her. She didn't feel like the Ragin' Cajun now. She felt like a little girl lost, just sitting tight while three older, wiser people tried to find the bully who kept picking on her.

"We understand you have a caller who threatens you every night," said Christina Anchor.

"Nothing we can't handle," Desirée told her.

"Really?" said Harris Cavanaugh. "So far, you haven't handled anything. That caller has been handling *you*."

"I hope you're a good investigator," retorted Desirée with a sneer, "because you aren't much of a diplomat."

"Look, Dez," said Kelvin, "they're here to help, so let's ease up a little on the attitude, OK?"

"We need to listen to the calls. I assume you have recordings?" asked Christina.

Kelvin smiled. "Of course. This is the digital age. We have all our hosts' shows on CDs. I keep copies in our archives."

"Go with him and listen," said Harris to Christina. "I'll take her statement now."

"OK."

"Remember what I said about your attitude," Kelvin admonished as he left the office with Christina. Desirée stayed seated as Harris stood over her.

"Smoke?" She took out a Pall Mall.

"Thanks, I just quit."

"You'll relapse."

He arched an eyebrow. "Are you always this charming?"

She smiled. "No, sometimes I'm a real bitch."

Harris looked around at the framed pictures of celebrities covering the walls. Robin Williams, Whoopi Goldberg, Arnold Schwarzenegger. Each of them had an arm around Desirée Dupree. "You have more friends than I do," he said.

"Surprise." She blew a smoke ring.

He toyed with the handle of her filing cabinet and she slapped his hand away. "Look but don't touch."

"Ouch."

She cocked her head to one side. "So...?"

He leaned against the filing cabinet and appraised her for a moment or two. "You aren't altogether the person I anticipated meeting."

She blew out a stream of smoke. "That's a damn shame."

"On the other hand, you *are* in some ways what I expected: sarcastic and unafraid to talk back to authority figures. I like your show overall, even if I find many of your political views highly"——he groped for the word——"unattractive. Of course, my impressions should be worth about thirty-five cents to you."

"Not even that much." She stubbed out her

cigarette. "So, let's get down to business."

"Yep." He took out his notepad, asked her questions and wrote down her answers, which were automatic and unhesitating.

"How long have you lived in San Francisco? A couple of years?" he asked.

"Yes."

"Have you made any enemies?"

She laughed. "Five nights a week. It's sort of my job."

"How about boyfriends? Broken anyone's heart lately?"

"No."

"Been dating at all?"

"No."

He arched an eyebrow. "No?"

"Do I stutter?"

He paused. "Just asking these questions because I need to know what's going on in your life. If a woman gets threatening phone calls, many times it's by a man she's rejected. Guys get a little bit nutso when that happens."

"Tell me about it."

"The man called you names that indicated sexual promiscuity—"

"I have no partner." Except myself, she added silently.

"Young women date," he observed.

"Not this one."

"Can you think of guys who've *wanted* to date you? Sometimes the most obsessive stalkers or harassers are those who can't even get the time of day from the people they're attracted to."

"No dates. No quickies. No nooners."

Harris got the impression that *he* wouldn't be able to get the time of day from her, either.

Desirée sighed and looked past Cavanaugh. "Remember Alan Berg, the Denver radio host who was gunned down some years back? He just did his thing, opening up the mike and saying what he thought. He got into on-air arguments all the time. He got rude. He made people angry. Some twisted neo-Nazi got so enraged that he killed Berg. Well, I get people angry, too. I am paid to provoke."

"Provocation doesn't justify harassment."

"Well, tell that to everyone out there in radio-land."

*Tough chick*, he thought. *That's how she's managed to thrive in broadcasting. Totally unafraid...or maybe she's just a scared little kid doing a great job of acting like a tough chick.*

"Right now," Harris told her, "you should be trying to remember what's been going on in the past few months. Have you been making personal appearances for KCA? Did anyone want an autograph or to shake your hand and you were just too busy for them? Such a trivial matter could make some people really irate. We have to narrow down our list of suspects. We can't simply go up to every male in the Bay Area and start throwing around accusations."

She grunted.

"I imagine you'd know the voice the moment you heard it," he said.

"Absolutely."

"How would you characterize it?"

She thought for a moment. "Creepy. Menacing. Breathless."

He paused. "Maybe I should hang out with you in the broadcast booth when you do your show."

Desirée frowned. "Are you *asking* or *telling* me?"

"That depends. If you say yes, I'm asking. If you say no, I'm telling. I have a badge. This is a criminal case. It's my call."

She lit another cigarette. "Next thing I know, you'll be moving in with me."

He let this pass. "Your shift starts at nine tonight, right? You should go home and take a nap. You look like walking death."

She snarled at him again. "Thanks."

Not that she wanted him to do so, but he walked her back to her car in the station's parkade, then reminded her to keep her doors locked in the car and at home. She found this cop nearly as chilling as the phone caller he was trying to catch.

In her car, she stopped and thought for a moment. What did he say his name was? Inspector Harris Cavanaugh. Desirée, a lifelong Clint Eastwood fan, remembered Eastwood as Inspector "Dirty" Harry Callahan in those cop movies from the 1970s.

Harris Cavanaugh. Harry Callahan.

She laughed. "Oh, my God," Desirée Dupree said out loud to herself. "I've got Dirty Harry on my case."

As Harris stood in the radio station's parking lot, he got a call on his Blackberry.

"So, Cavanaugh, what do you make of all this so far?" asked Christina Anchor at the other end.

"She's stubborn, egotistical, cynical and finds me totally repulsive." He chuckled. "This is gonna be fun."

# CHAPTER 2

"The difference between *running* for president and *being* president is negligible," the Ragin' Cajun said on the air. "Both involve going all over in limousines and having traffic blocked so you can get by. You stay in the very best hotels and make speeches and promise the American people things you can't deliver. You go through life believing that you're superior to everyone else. That's what's so terrible about it."

"It doesn't *sound* so terrible," said Don in Concord.

"But it *is* terrible. It indicates that one group of people is superior to everyone else and that such an elite is capable is solving everyone's problems. I have always believed that people, when left alone, are quite capable of running their own lives in a fulfilling way."

Harris had to admit that the lady knew what she

thought and had the poise to speak her mind in these most impersonal of surroundings—padded walls to minimize echoes, a computer screen listing the first names of callers and a big fuzzy phallus of a microphone sticking in her face. She leaned into the microphone as if having coffee with someone, as if it was just her and the person she was speaking to, or she pretended that Jay was listening to her. Desirée was lost in conversation, oblivious to—or at least not unnerved by—the fact that vast numbers of others were listening and that if her ratings slipped, Kelvin Barrow, her boss at KCA, would fire her in a heartbeat. She, more often than not, introduced the topic to be discussed and controlled the conversation by pressing the mute button whenever necessary. Mute button pressed, argument won.

Harris scratched his chin and pondered the enigma called the Ragin' Cajun. She sat perched on her seat, hostile, blunt, patronizing, probably like all the others in talk radio. Desirée, apparently, was just a little bit better at it than her competitors.

Bitchy was another word Harris was tempted to add in characterizing her. Ignorant, too; she hadn't acknowledged his presence all evening. Well, what of it? Cops were never popular, and Harris had even come to enjoy being someone people dreaded seeing. He liked his job; he liked putting together the pieces of the puzzle and putting the bad guy behind bars. He could handle people with attitudes. They were no trouble. Gunfire was big trouble. He tried to avoid it. He was successful most of the time.

Harris, throughout his life, had spent many gratifying hours reading Socrates, Plato and Kant but knew he couldn't have endured the day-to-day grind—or boredom—of being a psychologist or philosophy professor. Still, he had always been obsessed with life's largest questions. Who are we? What are we up to? He was damned if *he* knew.

He understood crime and its attractions. He knew that street drugs made people feel good and so did sex with a prostitute. He knew that people made lots of money through crime and that the best criminals often went unpunished. Harris was not naïve about these things; if he had made different choices in life, he himself might have become a criminal, dope addict or pimp.

But he was none of those things and he despised those who were. He wanted to catch the bad guy. That was his thing. He had discovered that the best way to catch the bad guys was to follow them around. Bad guys were compulsive; they kept acting bad over and over again, and in the end that's how the police were able to capture them.

Harris, occupying a corner of KCA's broadcast booth, alternated between looking out the huge windows at the San Franciscan night and staring at Desirée's shapely backside. She had a ferocious intellect and an aggressive sexiness in her voice that made her the girlfriend he had always wanted. She was a package that confounded him, made him want to get to know her better. But was she someone he ever could get to know?

She couldn't stand having him in there despite the studio's large size. She disliked having people around at work, period. Not even Jay, her engineer, who *had* to be on the other side of the glass to do his job. In a perfect world, she would do her show from the studio all alone. Certainly there would be no badly dressed cop sitting in the corner behind her gazing off into space, contemplating his navel or staring at her ass.

"Thanks for calling, Phil," she said to the guy from Sausalito. "We're approaching the top of the hour. The national news from New York is up next, then the local news. Then there'll be another hour of open phones with me, Desirée Dupree, here on KCA radio, Newstalk Nine-eighty."

She nodded at Jay, who switched over to the network news back east. The studio fell silent as Desirée turned down the volume. She took out a cigarette and lit it, then took several greedy hits.

"Do you *really* have to be here?" she asked Harris.

"Yes," he said. "Good show, so far."

"No thanks to you."

"I guess not."

"Say," she asked, "how long have you been a cop?"

"Fifteen years."

"You have the worst job in the world, Dirty Harry."

"No worse than yours."

Surprised at his answer, she turned around and looked at him. He had cold eyes, indeed. She didn't want to know about what he had seen and would see. She didn't want to know what he knew about crime and punishment. She wanted him to go away and take his bitter wisdom with him. She wanted to sit alone in her dark-hued cocoon and win arguments against people she couldn't see.

"If you agree that you have a crappy job, why do you stay with it?" she asked.

"Because it's the only thing I know how to do."

Desirée put her headphones back on and listened to the news. Harris let his mind wander, then gazed out at the Bay Bridge as it sparkled in the clear twilight. Quite a city. Nice neighborhood. He could remember when KCA was located in the Tenderloin, the highest-rated station in one of the city's most impoverished neighborhoods. Western Broadcasting had gone to much trouble and expense over building Broadcast House, now universally regarded as one of the city's least offensive new architectural wonders. That facility now housed Desirée Dupree, one of the city's most offensive new broadcasting wonders.

He also could make a decent guess as to how much it cost KCA to acquire her services, which was a hell of a lot more than *he* made. And it seemed as if every few minutes she was going to a newsbreak or commercials that went on forever. How much work did she actually *do* for those big paychecks?

By and by she came back on. "I am against censorship," she told Milt from Union City after he went on for a couple of minutes about the liberal justices of the Supreme Court. "I don't read *Hustler*. I don't visit Internet porn sites. I don't masturbate to erotic DVDs I bought online. But so what? Maybe *you* do, or someone else does. If your neighbor does, how is that any of *your* business? Or *mine*? This is supposed to be a free country; liberty and censorship are incompatible concepts. You can't have them both."

Harris smiled. For the moment she had forgotten about the harassing caller. But then she went on to the next one and the one after that. She frowned at the computer screen. "Jack in San Francisco, this is Desirée Dupree on KCA."

*Him?*

"Dezzzzirrrayyyy."

She shuddered and wanted to press the mute button. Harris leaned over to her and mouthed, *Talk.*

"What's on your mind, Jack?"

"*You're* on my mind. All the time. I'm gonna get you. I'm out here, waiting for you."

She swallowed hard. "Why do you want to get me?"

"Because of what you've done."

Desirée felt her insides caving in. "What have I done?"

"See? You don't even remember. You didn't care

enough about it, so you forgot. But I didn't."

The man's voice was low and nasal. She could imagine someone hideously ugly and utterly sinister somewhere out there, blaming her for some atrocity and hell-bent on punishing her for it.

"You will die, bitch. You will die."

Click.

Jay went to commercials. Harris took out his cell phone and made a call. "That was him," he said into the phone. "Did you trace him? I know he's in San Francisco. But where?"

Desirée, "Well...?"

Harris shook his head. "Not quite long enough."

She slumped forward. "Oh, Jesus."

"Don't worry. We'll get him. Or at least he won't get to you."

"The only thing I can say now is that I'm glad my show's over for the night. Now I can go home and have nightmares." Her mouth tasted of too many cigarettes and too much coffee. Her legs felt rubbery. "Maybe I should call my sister and have her come get me. I really don't trust myself to drive right now."

"Maybe," said Harris, "I should drive you home. No sense in bothering your sister."

"She bothers me all the time. I can bother her back. Sisters were made to be bothered——"

But Harris walked her briskly to his unmarked cruiser that was parked just outside the station's front entrance. He half-pushed her into the passenger's seat as he slipped behind the steering wheel.

"I don't like cops," she said.

"Me neither."

"Especially smug, condescending ones," she added.

"They're the worst kind."

"Especially the males who think they can push women around."

"All males are pure scum, period."

He pulled out on to Market Street and drove west as if needing no directions. She felt depleted, ready for a hot bath at home. What happened tonight was far scarier than anything she'd ever encountered in her career. Crank callers always seemed to be someone else's problem, or something the cops could end in a heartbeat. But, sitting here now with a police inspector, she knew he was, at least for now, powerless to stop the harassment. She felt safe as long as she had the police protection, but that wouldn't last forever.

"You're unorthodox, Dirty Harry," she said.

"So I've been told."

She was starting to annoy him. He didn't like it. He needed to be in control. Power struggles were things he liked to avoid. "Just cooperate with me and we'll catch this guy."

"I'm starting to think," she told him, "that maybe *you* won't make a hell of a difference one way or the other. And I'm thinking I don't want some showboating cop running my life. My boss brought you in. I am under no obligation to cooperate with you."

"The caller threatened your life on the air. That constitutes a criminal act. This whole case is no longer about your boss or your personal preferences regarding me. I'm here, you're here and we're gonna catch a creep. Understand?"

"OK." After some silence, she said, in a tiny, pleading voice, "Please stop the car for a moment."

He pulled over and she climbed out. He could hear her retching on the sidewalk. Soon she got back in. "Better there than in here," she said. "You wouldn't have gotten the smell out."

He grinned. If he had been angry at her a few minutes earlier—and he supposed he had—he wasn't now. It was difficult for him to stay mad at someone who had just vomited all over the sidewalk. He wanted to say kind things and tell her everything would be all right, but at the same time he didn't want to seem patronizing. He guessed she could immediately tell the difference between sincere concern and condescension.

"Want to go straight home or do you want to go somewhere else?" he asked.

"Straight home." She paused for a few moments and seemed somehow to regain her composure. "You've caught me at a bad time. Things were going great till the Voice from Hell started calling me. I shouldn't be giving you such a hard time, Dirty Harry. I know you're here to help."

"Why do you insist on calling me that?"

"Dirty Harry? Because you're the first San Francisco cop I've ever met named Harry, and you're a big guy like the other Dirty Harry." She pointed at his sportscoat. "I'll be you've got a forty-four Magnum in there, just like him. 'Most pow'ful handgun in the world. Can blow your head clean off.'"

"First of all," he said, "my name is Harris. No one

calls me Harry. Second, I don't carry a forty-four, just a three-fifty-seven."

"Whatever." Then, "This is really freaking me out. This whole thing has me pissing-my-pants terrified. He knows my work number. He knows my work address. Maybe he's been hacking into the DMV website and knows my home address, too."

"I very seriously doubt that."

"Why?"

"Because if he knew where you lived, he'd have visited you by now."

She smiled in spite of herself. "You're very comforting."

He shrugged. "I do my best."

They drove on for a few minutes. "You obviously have my address," she said.

"Wouldn't be much of an investigator if I didn't."

"You have the crappiest job in the whole wide

world. Why aren't you down in Los Angeles, acting in toothpaste commercials? You're handsome enough."

"I'll bet you say that to all the cops who protect you," he said.

She shook her head. "You're the first, Dirty Harry."

"God, I hate it when you call me that," he told her. "My name is Harris. Is that too difficult? Your name is Desirée. What do people call you? Dez?"

"Sometimes. The people who call me at work call me other things. As you've noticed."

"So, why do you dislike police?"

"That's for another time." Silence. "I am nocturnal. Working nine-to-five would drive me batty. Too many people out. Too much insanity. Too much traffic."

"The Ragin' Cajun versus the Human Race," Harris said.

She nodded. "Sometimes it seems that way."

Desirée at times wearied of listening to herself, telling others about her life. She talked for a living, so it was a nice change to shut up. People liked to talk about themselves, and she guessed Harris Cavanaugh wouldn't need a huge amount of prompting in that department. "So, Cavanaugh, are you a night owl, too?"

"For the time being. Thing about cop work is, they assign you to a specific shift. You don't like it, too bad. So I'm a nighttimer till they say otherwise."

"How do you like it so far?"

"It's definitely different."

She chuckled. "Well, yeah, it is that." Then, "Are you a native San Franciscan?"

"Yes, ma'am. Been here damn near every day of my life."

"This is my home now, too. I guess I'm here for life, and that's fine with me." New Orleans, Chicago,

Boston, now San Francisco. Now she had settled down. Monique was studying medicine at the University of California and, until that caller had started tormenting her, for Desirée and her sister life had become more or less routine, predictable.

"At least you'll be here as long as your ratings stay high and KCA keeps getting the big advertising bucks," Harris said.

Her eyes narrowed. "And why shouldn't they stay high?"

"It's just that one of the reasons you're so popular is that you're different from the local radio people. You're saying things the more conservative ones won't say and people tune in to hear what's gonna come out of the Ragin' Cajun's big mouth next. At some point they may get tired of you and stop listening. But I'm no expert."

"You're right," she said. "You're no expert."

They pulled up to her house. "Didn't mean to offend you. You have a nice home. Aren't you gonna ask me in for a martini?"

She unfastened her seatbelt. "Goodnight, Dirty Harry."

"What about your car? It's still at the radio station."

"So what? I'll take the bus in tomorrow and get it."

Harris was serious about being asked in. He wanted to see the inside of her home, to take her out for dinner and dancing. He bet she could eat like a horse and dance like a stripper. Then he would take her home and insist on a nightcap. He wouldn't give her the option of saying no. And they would be so busy with other things that they probably wouldn't get around to that nightcap.

She wasn't like the other women he had known. There probably would be no courtship between them, and what *did* happen would be spontaneous and temporary. Well, he'd been through *that* before. He would accept whatever he could get.

"In your busy schedule," he asked her, "is there ever any time for dinner?"

"Dinner?"

"Yeah, the last meal of the day for most people. I've been known to indulge in it myself. It's a great alternative to starvation."

Desirée frowned. "Are you asking me out on a date?"

"Maybe. If I *was* asking, what would you say?"

"I would say, 'Goodnight, Dirty Harry.'"

"But seriously...when do you eat?"

"Whenever I get hungry."

"Then we'll get hungry together."

She grew lightheaded, unsure of herself, annoyed at her reaction to this man and his cockiness. They weren't close at all, but she had let him get closer than she had let any other man in a long time. Or had *he* simply put her guard down without her even realizing it?

Whichever, she resolved to put her guard back up.

"You're very kind to invite me out, Inspector, but my answer is no."

"Mind if I ask why?"

"Oh, I think you already *know* why."

In the San Francisco police station, Harris stared at his computer screen, wishing the machine would simply do its own work. Its cursor just blinked at him, as if reminding him to quit wasting time and get busy. He observed, hardly for the first time, that the computer on his desk was a relatively new addition. A gift from the department: a widescreen monitor with almost painfully vivid graphics and a ludicrous storage capacity. Its predecessor, removed by the Toshiba geeks who had installed the current system, had been less sleek and shiny but perfectly functional. The Microsoft weasles had been by, too, fixing what wasn't broken. What, Harris wanted to know but did not ask, did his brand-new machine have that his older ones didn't? Perhaps it was true, as he had heard, that California's law-enforcement bosses, learning that authorities in Nevada or Arizona had upgraded their hardware, concluded that the Golden State couldn't exist without shiny new gadgets, either.

Harris craved a cigarette but knew if he bummed one from the cop fifteen feet away, he would be too disgusted with himself to enjoy the smoke.

His problem with motivation at the moment was Desirée Justine Dupree. Ordinarily he was the most disciplined cop he knew, largely unaffected by the chaos he encountered each workday. A police psychiatrist would find him totally and refreshingly free of mental and physical illnesses, divorces and addictions. Well, nicotine for him *was* an addiction, but the shrink would be delighted that Harris had quit smoking.

But for now he could not get his mind off Desirée. There were plenty of distractions, of course; if there was one thing San Francisco did not lack, it was criminals and the work they generated for people like Harris Cavanaugh.

As phones rang, heels clicked and voices sounded, Harris' mind kept flashing back to the radio station in which he and his partner, Christina Anchor, had recently spent so much time. He had been gratified to see Desirée warm up to and confide in him. He also suspected that maybe she had even begun to reciprocate his liking for her.

Of course, maybe that was in his imagination. Desire clothed in thought, as Socrates would have said. Harris knew one thing: trying to stop thinking about Desirée would accomplish nothing. His obsession with her—if one could call it that—would have to run its course.

Harris had had enough experience to know about the complicated, irrational games women and men frequently played with each other. Throughout his life he had been attracted to women who did not want him, and vice versa. Rejection was less devastating to him now than before. He simply assured himself she wasn't the woman for him, though his emotions sometimes insisted otherwise. He often reminded himself of the old saying,

"Women are like buses; another comes along every fifteen minutes."

Well, he didn't give a damn about that next woman who was due in fifteen minutes. He wanted the one currently occupying his mind. He couldn't imagine wanting anybody else.

Inevitably, these thoughts made him mentally review her case. The caller continued threatening Desirée during every shift. KCA's call-in lines were notoriously jammed by listeners eager to have at it with the host, yet Desirée's tormentor always got through, which meant he probably had a Demon Dialer. Harris believed there was still every chance that the caller would tire of the harassment and find other amusements, since physically stalking someone was infinitely more difficult than just making phone threats. But as long as the guy persisted, the police needed to take the matter seriously.

Harris and Christina had crept around, checking the usual suspects who'd been charged with using the phone to harass ex-girlfriends. Then the cops had confidentially interviewed Desirée's colleagues and probed as deeply as they could into many aspects of Desirée life since her arrival in the Bay Area. They had come up with nothing, which surprised Harris very little.

So the investigation continued. Harris hit a key or two and Desirée's résumé appeared on his screen. The document told him much about her, as the facts of a person's life often did.

Harris chuckled. New Orleans, Chicago, Boston, San Francisco. Packing and unpacking, up and down the dial. That's showbiz, folks. Desirée had been one of the luckier voices-for-hire, starting in a big city and making it to San Francisco before age thirty. Radio personalities nearly twice her age hadn't gone half as far. Half those people also had master's degrees in broadcasting, while Desirée, so far as Harris knew, had never even set foot on a college campus. What had she said about herself on the air? "No B.A., no B.S." Maybe *that* was her secret.

"Having fun?" Christina Anchor stood over him.

Harris looked up at her. "I've just been looking at the Dupree file. What do you make of her?"

"She's not *my* idea of an evening's stimulating entertainment. Ballsy lady, though. Smart. Is there *anything* the Ragin' Cajun *doesn't* know?"

Harris gave her a small, twisted smile. "Yeah. She doesn't know who's harassing her."

Christina pointed at the can of cashews on Harris's desk. "May I?"

"Help yourself."

She looked at the can. "'Imported gourmet cashews. Roasted and salted.'" Christina picked out a couple of jumbo-sized nuts and popped them into her mouth. "Yummy! Got a cold beer to go along with these?"

"Drinking while on duty? That's very intelligent, Anchor."

"Anyway, about Desirée Dupree. She *seems* to be made of iron...but inside she's just shuddering. She knows this caller may not go away. She's terribly insecure."

Harris guffawed. "Her? Insecure? I seriously doubt that."

"Dahlinks, she's in *showbiz*. She's a *performer*. She's insecure as hell and in her mind she'll never be good enough. That's what drives her to be as good as she is." She went back to the cashews. "Want any more insights into female behavior, I'm your gal."

"Give me my nuts back," Harris said. She handed the can back and he popped a cashew into his mouth. "If you're right about her insecurity, I'll take you to dinner Masa's."

She smirked. "Gee, then I guess I better go home after work and pick out something nice to wear."

"Can you believe this jerk calls her *every* night? We better kick up our investigation into the next gear."

"She hasn't been the most cooperative person. It's like she thinks he'll just go away eventually." She frowned. "I don't think he will."

"Nope. So we should intensify things a little bit. I'm going to be sitting in with her tonight, so why don't you get on the phone to Atlanta? Her boss or anyone else who knew her. Her landlord. We'll see what we can get."

"And we better get something soon or this will soon become a low-priority case." She made a face. "Which means you won't be able to hang out at the KCA studio and ogle your ladylove."

Before he could make a retort, his phone rang. He picked it up and spoke his name.

*"Dirty Harry,"* she said.

He was too alarmed at the terror in her voice to feel annoyed at that nickname. "Desirée—?"

*"He called me at home. He knows my number "Hurry,"* she said.

"I'm already there."

# CHAPTER 3

Desirée seemed almost apologetic by the time Harris and Christina reached her house. A phone call, she reminded herself, was not the same as having the maniac at her front door.

She also reminded herself that she was a professional broadcaster. She could handle difficult people. What she needed now, she decided, was to make the caller think she was indifferent to him and his pranks. *Then* maybe he would get frustrated and go away.

Desirée's father had been the most diplomatic of men. He believed that a sadist could be stripped of his power by being ignored or mocked. Her mother had observed that punches and kicks could be effective as well. Desirée decided they were both right, but that in this case she would use ignorance and mockery.

Of course, she hadn't handled *this* call that way. She had gotten enraged and started threatening *him*—she had the cops on his ass and if he bugged her again he would be hung by his scrotum—and she now felt that was precisely the reaction he had wanted. She worried about Monique. Would her sister answer the next time the maniac called?

She paced about her living room, her heart pounding, her pulse racing, her mind full of panic. She had cut off the caller in mid-sentence, slammed down the phone and bolted the door. Gazing up at her majestically high ceilings and arched entryways, she felt safe, as if the grand old house's thick white walls had taken her into their protective embrace.

Desirée and Monique had arrived in San Francisco with just a couple of suitcases. They had stayed at a hotel at first, and now had stylishly old-fashioned-looking new furniture in their spacious home. Their living expenses were high, yes, and they now had little walking-around money. But every time Desirée looked at her new home or watched her sister drive off to medical school, she knew these huge expenditures had been worthwhile.

Desirée at the age of twenty-nine had certainly made a comfortable home for herself and Monique, and she was damned if she would let some deranged loner interfere with her stability.

She pondered her options. She believed they were dwindling. The importance of the maniac's phone call was that he wouldn't quit. He was just getting started. He was moving closer. She would be a fool to pretend otherwise. She was fighting him the only way she could: through the cops. But how much could they do? She supposed she could only go to work as usual and take his abuse with Dirty Harry or that bossy-as-hell woman Anchor standing over her, trying to trace the maniac's calls. Eventually Dirty Harry probably would nail him and the caller would turn out to be some Charles Manson-type weirdo who claimed the Ragin' Cajun was controlling his thoughts.

*Bitch. Slut. Whore. You die soon. Understand? You die soon.*

Just then she heard her phone. "Desirée? It's Harris. We're parked right outside your front door. We're coming up right away. Don't panic."

Opening the door for them, Desirée watched Christina Anchor look around with poorly hidden envy as the two police inspectors stepped into the Ragin' Cajun's living room with its high ceiling, artisan's cherubs and curlicues and arched entryways.

"Nice place," said Anchor. They all sat in the living room. Desirée folded her arms across her chest. Harris sat on a sofa so huge that it ran nearly the width of one of the considerable walls.

"This was the first time the guy has called me at home," Desirée said, as if still unable to believe that her privacy had been so invaded.

"Do you remember what he said?" Christina asked.

"Yes." She closed her eyes and said things that Harris, the most case-hardened of law-enforcement professionals, found almost impossible to believe, especially when hearing such filth in Desirée's silky, familiar voice.

Christina Anchor, swallowed hard, looking ready to vomit. "You, uh, have a good memory."

Desirée shrugged. "I've been in broadcasting for years. A good memory is an asset."

"Like all public figures, you have an unlisted phone number. Who *does* have yours?" Harris asked.

"Actually, we have three phones. The land line here on the table, which the caller used. Plus, my sister and I each have a cell phone. The radio station has my land line number, the medical school, my lawyer and a few personal friends." She paused and ran a nervous hand through her hair. "This latest call means that the guy can also get our address—"

Just then the front door swung open.

Desirée frowned. "Monique? What are *you* doing here?"

"I live here." The woman looked at the cops with large, angry hazel eyes. "You're here about the caller, right?"

Harris nodded.

"Sis, I thought you had a seminar or something to go to," Desirée said, her voice soft but obviously full of anger.

"I did."

"Then why aren't you *at* the seminar?"

"Just can it, OK? You know, the other stations in town are covering this story. 'Ragin' Cajun harassed by caller.' Dez, I thought you said the cops were on it and everything was cool."

Desirée gave her sister a sweet, patronizing little smile and said, "Well, the cops *are* on it and everything *is* cool."

"Oh, I'm sure," Monique said.

To Harris, the two Dupree women resembled each other enough, especially around the eyes and mouth, that if they were standing far apart in a crowded room, it would take him only a minute or so to figure out that they were sisters. While Desirée was attractive and could have looked much better with a moderate amount of effort, Monique was a knockout who demanded to be taken seriously despite her beauty. So far, she was getting plenty of respect.

Monique was dressed in sweaters, pleated slacks and boots. College-girl attire for San Franciscans. She had short dark hair and almost no makeup. Desirée dressed strictly for comfort: gym suits, sneakers, T-shirts. Her hair was held in place with a ribbon. She looked good in spite of herself. She had an inherent sexiness despite her dubious fashion sense.

Besides their family name, Harris thought, they shared a feisty temperament. Neither woman would take crap from anyone, least of all the other. And when one got in the other's face, well, it was better than female mud wrestling on TV.

Christina shot Harris a look that said, *It's showtime, folks.*

He shot back a look that said, *Get for a pizza and crack open a six-pack.*

But the fun ended before it began. Monique said, "You're impossible. Totally impossible." She turned to Harris and said, "My sister's an idiot. Are *you* an idiot, too?"

"Excuse me?" Harris couldn't quite believe what he had just been asked.

"Nevermind." To Christina, "Would you update me on the case, please?"

"We're trying to catch the caller. We're trying to make progress."

"Why are you here right now?" Monique asked. Then, with a speed that made Harris think she should become an investigator instead of a doctor, Monique pointed at their home phone and said, "Did he call *this* number?"

When Harris nodded, Monique groaned.

"C'mon, don't sweat it," Desirée said. "The cops are here. They'll put things right."

"Yes," Christina said. "We're making progress. We'll catch the culprit as soon as we can." She reached inside her jacket pocket and took out her cell phone. Then she went into the hallway for privacy.

"Coffee," Monique muttered, disappearing into the kitchen.

Desirée and Harris remained in the living room. Harris said, "Your sister is an attractive young lady."

"She's not your type."

Harris grinned. "How do you know?"

"I just do." Then, "Your partner—*she* seems your type."

"Well, we just work together. We're not getting married."

Desirée said nothing. She didn't like bringing up

81

the subject of Christina Anchor. By nature Desirée had always considered herself every man's equal and every woman's competitor...and now Superwoman was unable to manage her own trouble. So the cops came in to help, and who did they send? A tall, good-looking, intelligent woman inspector. Anchor, Desirée realized, with some resentment, was one squared-away chick. And Desirée tried not to hate her for it.

"Coping OK so far?" Harris asked.

Desirée shrugged. A lot you've done so far.

He leaned towards her and spoke firmly. "We're gonna catch him. You gotta *keep the faith.* Understand?"

She nodded. "Understood." In truth, she wanted to be away from Dirty Harry and Christina Anchor. She wanted to pack up, leave this city and take Monique back with her to the Big Easy. Forget about all this ugliness. But that was not an option.

"Just one thing," she said. "This is *my* problem,

not my sister's. I want to keep it that way."

Harris nodded. "Yeah, we can arrange police protection for her."

"Thanks. Like I said, it's *my* problem."

"Soon it won't be *anyone's* problem."

When had any man shown her any empathy? When had she needed any? She looked away, not wanting to let this big cop see her this vulnerable. She really wanted to crawl into his lap and go to sleep for a few years. Instead she said, "I've gotta get to work soon."

"Can't you call in sick? I've noticed they always have a replacement ready."

She stood up and put her hands on her hips. "Then the maniac would know he was the reason I'd called in sick. No thanks, no way."

"Doesn't the Ragin' Cajun ever give herself a break?"

She squared her shoulders. He was moving in on

her, absorbing her substance. She wanted to run but he was her sanity. Panic shot through her. Stubbornness kept her shoulders squared, her head up. He was easing his way into her world and he knew it, the bastard. He knew it as surely as he knew his own name. He was a patient man and he would just keep easing, easing. He was wearing her out.

"Back off a little, Cavanaugh," she said.

Soon, very soon, he would take her into his arms and remind her of man-woman love. What it was, what it could truly be.

"'Back off'? No can do, Dupree."

She sneered. "I wasn't asking, I was telling."

He was tempted to bounce her across the room and through the huge picture window. But he just shook his head, saying nothing.

Monique marched in as if she'd heard their exchange, which she probably had. "Coffee, guys."

The two murmured thanks. Monique said, "I'm in

for the rest of the night. To her sister, she said, "From now on you may call me Dr. Dupree."

"I'll call you whatever I want as long as I'm paying your tuition."

"I mean it," Monique said with mock gravity. "I want you to call me Dr. Dupree or Your Highness."

"On that note," said Desirée, "I think it's time for me to head off to the station to prepare for tonight's show."

Harris jumped up and met her at the front door.

"What's going on?" Desirée asked.

"We're going to work." Harris waved at Monique as he and Desirée went out the door.

...

"We have to stop meeting like this," Desirée said as she and Harris waited in the radio station's parking lot for the elevator. "I really don't need you holding my hand in the damn studio each night I work."

The elevator door swung open and Desirée let out a whelp, then stepped back and slammed into Harris. "Dang, Jimmy, what am I gonna *do* about you!"

"Oops! Beg your pardon, Miz Dupree!" The electrician had thinning hair and a skeletal body. On his blue workshirt the name Jimmy was spelled on an oval patch. "I take the elevator so much, I forget that whenever I'm going out, someone's maybe coming in."

"Don't mind me," she said. "Not my best week."

"I understand." He pointed to his toolbelt. "One thing you don't have to worry about is being electrocuted while I'm around."

Desirée smiled. "Glad to hear it. You gonna listen in tonight?"

He nodded. "I'll do my best." He stepped past them, his delicate gait labored.

Harris and Desirée settled into her office. She took a yellow legal pad and started scribbling down potential topics for that night's show. Harris sat in the other chair.

"Tonight? Hmm. So much wrong in the world, so little airtime for me."

"What about the Iraq war?" Harris asked.

"Everyone else is doing it. Still, it's an interesting issue. Especially the financial end. Costing way too much. Our dollar is down against all the other major currencies."

"How about terrorism?"

Desirée nodded. "That's always good. Especially if the other hosts have neglected it for a day or two. I asked the listeners once if they thought we should rebuild the World Trade Center just as it was. They said no. It was on haunted land. Nobody would move back into that place and they know it."

"Sky marshals on flights?"

"Oh, I'm sure they've been on board since nine-eleven. They probably have handguns in the cockpits now, too."

"Arnold Schwarzenegger. How's he been as governor?"

Desirée laughed. "A lot better than people would have guessed. Conan the Terminator running California, right? A big joke, and Californians love jokes. But he is a very astute businessman, and that's what we've needed. The liberals want to spend money the government doesn't have."

"Some of the things you say on the air," Harris said, shaking his head. "I can't believe your bosses let you get away with that."

Desirée shrugged. "Well, they do. For now, anyway."

Soon they were in the studio while Ernie Ford finished up. Ernie was a spectacularly corpulent man with a great head of gray hair. One of the city's most respected broadcasters, he had been glad KCA hired Desirée. The station was too conservative, he said, and he was its most conservative host. Desirée had a sexy voice and a headful of way-out ideas—just what the station needed for balance.

Ernie looked up at her and smiled. "You still ragin', Cajun?"

She smiled. "As always."

"Well, this nightmare will be over before you know it." To Harris he said, "Hey, copper."

Harris nodded. Despite his conservative views, Ernie Ford had been most critical of the San Francisco Police Department, knowing that most of his listeners had had at least one bad experience with the cops, if only a traffic ticket. The police were always an easy target for talk-show hosts, and Ernie was out for high ratings. Harris and the other cops considered him no friend of theirs.

Desirée settled in behind the mike and watched the activity on her computer screen as Harris sat in a swivel chair by the window. Newsbreaks, commercials. Then came KCA's unmistakable jingle and Desirée opened up the microphone and said, as naturally as if teasing her kid sister, "Get ready for three hours of the most provocative radio on the West Coast. The voice of KCA can be heard from Mexico to Canada...in fact, if you have a computer with Internet access, you can hear us from just about wherever you are in the world. And we're going to start this evening with an hour of open lines. So if you've got something to talk about—doesn't matter what—pick up the phone and have your say. There are potentially millions of people tuning in at this moment, more people than you will ever meet, and they are waiting to hear what you think. I have lines open on the board. Our number is 800-555-2KCA."

She closed the mike and said in Harris' direction, "By the way, my boss wants to give you a KCA windbreaker as a thank-you for your help. It has the station's logo in huge letters on the back for everyone to admire."

"You mean for everyone to laugh at. Forget the windbreaker. I would much rather have a date with you. Dinner and dancing. When are you free?"

"Give it up, Dirty Harry."

A commercial came on for Boccasio's Jewelers on Union Square, the same one that Harris had heard for what seemed a zillion years.

Desirée turned down the volume.

Harris said, "Thank you."

"For what? I just broke your heart by turning you down for dinner and dancing."

"I was thanking you for turning down that damn commercial. I *hate* that commercial. This station has been playing it since I was a college kid."

"You've heard that spot too many times. That's why you hate it."

"No, I hate it because it's a dumb commercial. I've always hated it. Know what? I can't help but hear that awful commercial every time I pass Boccasio's."

She chuckled. "I think that's the point."

Soon the break was over and she went back on the air. Ted in Redwood City said, "Aren't you glad Barry Bonds finally broke Hank Aaron's home-run record?"

"No, but I'll be glad when Alex Rodriguez breaks Bonds's record. Sorry, guy, but I have no admiration for juicers."

Desirée was acutely aware of Harris in the corner near the window. How could she concentrate on slamming Barry Bonds when Dirty Harry was checking her out? She could feel the vibrations emanating from him. Vibrations of masculine strength and intense interest.

Well, he would just have to find another woman. She wasn't available to him. She wasn't available to anyone. Desirée wanted only for Harris Cavanaugh to do his job and be gone. She had come out here not to sleep with him, but to do a nightly radio show. They paid her top dollar to keep the phone lines jammed and the ratings high. She had held her own and then some—and if she failed, she would be out on her ear, just like all the others over the years who had come on board, done their very best and then very quietly disappeared from KCA because they just couldn't deliver the goods. Success was hers only as long as she made it her top priority.

So she resolved to forget about Harris. He was a handsome man. He could get other women. Why bother with *her?*

In a few moments another long series of commercials and other messages started. Desirée started having crazy images of herself at the microphone, perched on Harris' lap, his thighs solid as stone, his face seeking hers. She felt his finger tracing her delicate jawline, his kiss just moments away, his desire growing unmistakable beneath her. She squirmed, feeling the studio's walls closing in on her, Harris' iron embrace squeezing the breath from her lungs.

As if hearing her thoughts, he moved his chair closer to hers. Part of his plan had been to tease her out of the high anxiety she lived with because of the menacing caller. Upon getting to know her, he sensed that, despite her remarkable popularity among radio listeners and the goodwill from her station colleagues—goodwill that could become dismissal as soon as her ratings slipped, which at any point could very easily happen. Desirée needed a friend, aside from her sister, and Harris wanted to become that confidant. If she would only let him. And if she did, that she would be more than he could handle.

He sat inches away from her in the studio and looked at her, thinking of moonlit walks along Fisherman's Wharf, drives across the Golden Gate Bridge and mornings together at his place or hers, snuggling and making plans for the day. What man could resist a woman who made him think of such things?

Not ethical, Harris reminded himself. Not professional. Remember where you are and why. He eased himself out of the  chair and left the studio. Desirée, with minutes to spare till she was back on the air, did the deep-breathing exercises she had been practicing for years. She had read Buddhist books and listened to Ram Dass tapes about yoga, meditation and other ways of getting drugless highs.

What made Dirty Harry run? He was a police investigator who read Socrates for fun. He had a dimestore wardrobe and a million-dollar mind. She didn't feel comfortable around people who were walking contradictions, partly truth and partly fiction.

Well, she wouldn't have to be around him much longer if he did his job and caught his perp. He was a cop and a man—two qualities that disqualified him from having any place in her personal life. If he wanted a woman, why didn't he hook up with that partner of his, the tall gung-ho lady Christina Anchor? She seemed to have eyes for him, teasing him all the time. Maybe he should investigate her instead of Desirée.

The national news began. Top of the hour. Desirée thought again about how well everything had fallen into place in the past couple of years. Her career had vastly surpassed her expectations. Desirée was bohemian—her artistic temperament was incompatible with rigidly disciplined work. She was completely self-taught, unfettered by the rigors of a formalized education. In contrast, her sister Monique, never a square peg, was born for college and a conventional career.

Looking for solace in difficult times years earlier, Desirée had found Buddhism. She didn't go to dharma halls or Zen centers but she did read *Be Here Now* on a regular basis. She learned that everything was temporary; nothing lasted. Her present troubles would soon vanish. Things would quiet down for a time; maybe the hard times would return. All Desirée Dupree could do was her best. Savor the good, endure the bad. It helped to remind herself of this a few hundred times per day. She came back on the air to remind her listeners to keep listening, then it was back to commercials and newsbreaks. She got up and walked across the studio, out of Jay's line of sight, to stretch.

Just then Harris came in. She didn't hear his entrance as she stood facing the huge studio windows, moving to music only she could hear.

"I haven't seen moves like that since I stopped

hanging out at the North Beach bump-and-grind joints," Harris said.

She whirled around, blushing.

"Just thought you might be thirsty," he said, tossing her a can of iced tea he'd just bought from the hallway vending machine. "It's much better for you than coffee."

She opened her can. "We're not supposed to drink or eat in the broadcast booth."

"So we won't tell anyone."

"Frankly, right now I would rather have an ice-cold beer."

Harris smirked. "Seems to me there are FCC rules about the consumption of alcoholic beverages while on the air." Then he added, "It's nearly time," meaning that her shift was almost over and that the maniac caller had failed to get through or had stopped trying altogether.

"Still got an hour to go," she said. "We're not out

of the woods yet."

"If he calls, try to keep him on the line. That's all you can do. We're all hooked up with Jay in the control booth to trace the caller. And if he does call, keep pelting him with questions. That really appeals to his ego."

"Harris, how much longer are you going to be here with me? I mean, the police department can't afford it, right? At some point I'll have to deal with this guy on my own."

"Not necessarily. If I'm half as good as I think, we're just about to catch this guy."

From the booth, Jay gestured that Desirée had two minutes. Both she and Harris stayed silent as the last commercial ended and her mike went live.

"Dave in Santa Clara, this is Desirée Dupree on KCA."

"Dez, I've heard so much about 'smart guns.' Why aren't they being used yet by the police?"

"Because they're actually *dumb* guns. The inventor tried to make a gun that could be fired only by its owner. The handle of the gun contains a computer chip that communicates with a sensor worn like a wristwatch by the gun's owner. When the gun and the sensor get too far apart, the gun locks up.

"The problem is that they were trying to marry high tech with low tech. Gun powder and computer chips don't mix. Another problem is that when these guns get dropped, they tend to stop working. I would say that most cops out there would be very reluctant to use a smart gun, when the regular, old-fashioned ones do just fine."

She paused. "Tom in Modesto..."

He wanted to talk baseball. The A's and Giants. She was game. Then Brad from Richmond wanted to talk about the latest Hollywood bimbos who had been pulled over for DUIs.

"Clyde in San Francisco, this is Desirée Dupree—"

"Dezzzzirrraaayyyy."

She looked up at Harris, who nodded for her to switch to commercials. She did and said to the caller, "Clyde, why do you keep changing your name?"

"Nevermind. You will die soon. You know that?"

"I think you're bluffing. If you haven't offed me yet, it means you can't. You're full of crap."

She didn't feel Harris's hands massaging her shoulders as the caller spat a stream of invective at her.

"You got quite a vocabulary," she said. "You must've gone to college to learn all those four-letter words."

"You killed my friend," said the caller, now clearly on the verge of furious tears. "You manipulated him and destroyed his life. Now you pay with yours."

"Who?" Desirée demanded. "I didn't take advantage of anyone. Come out and say your name and——"

Click.

Harris took out his cell phone. "Get him this time?" He swore and said, "We'll get him next time, Desirée. He's flat-out psychotic. He'll keep at it till we get him. Maybe he wants to be caught."

Just then Matt McDonald came in.

"Yeah? What do you want?" snapped Harris.

"Uh, I just thought I would see if everything's OK."

"Everything's fuckin'-A great," said Harris.

"I'm fine, Matt," Desirée said. "What would really be great is if you guys would just leave me in peace." She looked at her monitor and hit a switch. "Mel in Hayward, you're on the air with the Ragin' Cajun..."

...

Midnight arrived, eventually. Desirée got through the final hour with little discomfort and decided that she was learning to deal with the menacing caller. Just go to commercials and keep the cretin on the line. Cavanaugh and his crew could nab the guy and Desirée could get on with her life.

Harris insisted on driving her home in her own car.

"How will you get back to KCA to get your own car back?" she asked. "You know I live far away."

"I'll hitchhike."

By and by they reached her house through rolling fog. Desirée decided she lived in perhaps the creepiest neighborhood in San Francisco.

"Home, sweet home," Harris said.

"No place like it," she said.

"You've got a nice big sofa in your living room," he remarked as he parked the car. "I'm gonna sleep on it tonight."

She shrugged. "Whatever turns you on." Sitting in parked cars at night always emboldened her. She lit a cigarette. "You know, tonight taught me something. I don't need your help that much. I can deal with this creep on my own."

"Really? I gotta hear this. Tell me more."

"Well, my guess is that it's a case of misplaced rage. This is San Francisco. Maybe his boyfriend left him and he's taking it out on me." She laughed. "I just have to straighten his ass out, so to speak."

"Just gonna straighten him out? Simple as that?"

"Yeah. Look, he keeps calling me exploiter and manipulator and all those filthy names. I'm just not gonna take any more of his crap—"

"Dez, do you remember what I said to you when we first met? You insisted that you could handle this guy on your own. I said that *he's* been handling *you* and *you* couldn't handle *him*. Well, nothing's changed much. He's sociopathic. He's got this little drama happening with you and he has to play it out. My job is to play it out with him and put him behind bars so he can't play out these little dramas with anyone else."

She grunted. "He probably thinks I'm some sort

of glamorous media personality who seduces her public. Truth is, I'm a muckraker. I provoke the rubes into calling me to tell me I'm full of crap. But once they get on the air, I just press the mute button to shut them up. Then I repeat my argument and hang up. Therefore, I win." She sighed. "It's all very sick and twisted—"

"But it pays well," Harris said.

Desirée laughed in spite of herself. "I guess I'm experiencing one of the hassles of public life. Someone fixates on you and gets obsessed." She added, "He gets obsessed with someone who hasn't had a date lately and couldn't even keep a marriage together."

Harris arched an eyebrow. "Married...?"

"I thought you knew that. Haven't you been sticking your nose into my personal business?"

"Well, apparently I missed that fact. A difficult fact to miss on Google." He shook his head. "I did a search on you and didn't find out that you were divorced. Shame on me. Shame on Google."

"It's almost not worth mentioning. When I was still in my teens, I married a guy named Bob LaPorte."

"Where is he now? Still in New Orleans?"

She shrugged. "So far as I know." She dragged on her cigarette. "But this caller...is so far beyond any kook I've ever encountered in broadcasting. Wow."

"Welcome to the Golden State of California."

"The last guy I dated said I was as frigid as a glacier. Maybe I should give his number to the weirdo caller. Those guys would have something to talk about."

"I think," Harris said in the darkness, "that you need to grow up."

"Come again?"

"Grow up. Sure, in some ways you've matured. You're not yet thirty and you've succeeded in a business that chews up and spits out people much older than yourself. But in your personal life, you can't have a symbiotic, mature relationship with a man. You still seem to think all men are like the guys who call in to your show. You can just press the mute button and then hang up on them."

Desirée glowered at him. "I'm putting my sister through medical school. I'm buying this nice big house we live in and I'm doing it all without anyone's help."

"I repeat: You need to grow up."

She sneered. "Fuck you very much."

He laughed. "I'm no shrink. I'm just a cop. And a man. And I know what I see when I look at you."

"Tell you what," Desirée said, opening the door and getting out. "You just do your thing and catch this creep, OK?"

He got out too. "OK. But right now, let's go inside and try something. Just to see how it goes."

She eyed him. "Like what?"

# CHAPTER 4

In Desirée's living room, Harris held her by the arms. "Just to confirm that you have no use for men in general and me in particular."

She reached up, as if to push him away, but left her hands clawing at his lapels. Standing so close to him, she was amazed at the vast wall of his chest and his formidable height. She swore she could feel his heart hammering in his chest, then realized it was her own heartbeat; his was even and normal.

"This is ludicrous," she said.

"So it is." He smiled. "Do you feel you're into something you can't control?"

He saw that he was right about her. He had provoked her in just the right way. All that mattered to him was that she reacted to him in some way.

She looked up at him and let her hands find their way up to his shoulders. He showed no expression. He simply wanted to see what was coming next.

That was his thing, she thought. Provocation. Well, she could teach him a few things. She brought his head down and kissed his lips. They were smooth and dry, indifferent.

She pulled back and asked, "How was that?"

"I've had better," he lied. His voice sounded utterly without emotion. "You're out of practice, Cajun," he said, letting his hands settle onto her hips. "You want to work on that with me a little? We've got the rest of the night."

Desirée snarled at him. She wanted to slap his face, spit into his eyes. Instead, she yanked his head down again and tried harder. Much harder.

His lips were much as they were seconds earlier, but now they devoured her. For the briefest moment panic seized her—she wanted to run from him, to sprint out the door and into the street. But the moment passed and she felt suddenly full of passion, wild wonderful horrible passion, needs neglected for so long now assertive themselves, taking her over, turning her inside out. She grabbed at him and clawed at him, her fingernails digging into his neck, the woman claiming the man, wanting nobody else and allowing him no other woman. She took him and made him hers, remembering what she had vowed to forget so many times. Remembering, remembering...

Her mind went mercifully, marvelously blank. She could feel the endless whole of him, the reassuring strength of his arms as they explored her waist, her back, her hair. His mouth pressed into hers, wanting more than he could have, more than she could ever give.

He knew she was dangerous. A woman, starved of loved, now tasting the nectar of passion. He told himself he could handle it. Sitting in the studio with her or sitting at his desk alone, his professional concentration sometimes failed and he had fantasized about her, about this moment with her.

He had fantasized about holding her against him, feeling her narrow length, hearing her moans of pleasure, inhaling the scent of her.

But now he was with her. Now it was happening. And it was far, far more than he could ever have been prepared for.

She was like gasoline, clear and deadly. She poured herself into him, splashing through him, filling every cell in his body until he wanted to pull away and beg her to stop. Or did he? Did he want their loving to continue forever, did he want to disregard everything else...?

She moaned and grabbed, unable to decide what she wanted. More? Less? She tried to pry herself from his iron grip but he held on, not ready yet to give her up.

In a moment he released her. He wanted to look into her eyes, to see what had just happened to them both, to see all their feelings in her eyes. And he saw just what he wanted and expected to see, the moist yearning that also filled his being, her quivering lips that ached for more of him.

"Round two," he murmured, pulling her against his chest and continued.

She wanted no more. She wanted to be apart from him now, to sit alone and ponder. Or did she? No. She gave in to the feelings that enveloped her, feelings every color of the rainbow and every texture she liked, feelings she could not have willed away with all her effort. While she was in his arms, reason stood no chance. She became gasoline again, liquid and fiery, spilling into her man, setting him aflame.

He could never have enough. All of her ten times over would be too little. He craved her body, mind, soul, spirit—he needed it all. He kissed her for eternities, his mouth exploring the delightful secrets in hers, the rest of him burning for the secrets her body had yet revealed to him. He wanted to learn those secrets. He wanted to spend the rest of his life discovering all there was to find out about this woman, and he guessed it would take the rest of his life.

He needed more now. He slipped his hands underneath her sweater and fondled her breasts. Yum!

"Let's cool off a bit," she said, leading him to the sofa.

"Good idea."

They sat a respectable distance apart. She ran a hand nervously through her hair and looked around at the wide, oval-shaped living room that was the closest thing to a permanent home she'd had in some time, and certainly the most comfortable one. She wondered if there was any way she could convince herself that this kiss with Harris had never happened. Never underestimate the power of denial, as the radio shrinks had so often said.

She took a deep breath and said, "That was inappropriate."

He smirked. "Worse things have been done by better people."

"You mock me."

"You take yourself too seriously."

"Dammit, Harris——"

He pointed at her. "That was the first time you've ever called me by my name. So this evening hasn't been a total write-off." He leaned in closer. "I guess from now on you'll call me Harris. Right?"

"Wrong." She sprang to her feet, as if to get the advantage by looking down at him. "Maybe I should call the police and have what's-her-name take over for you. Inspector Boyle."

"Her name's *Anchor*——and it's *our* case. You can't just call the police and say, 'I don't like cop you've sent, so send me a different one.'" He sat back and watched her pace in front of him, eager to hear her reply and wishing that she would change into something less baggy and more clingy, the better to show off her breasts and hips.

"I didn't think that at all," Desirée lied. She continued walking in front of him, not altogether minding his rapt attention to her breasts and bottom but also wanting him to observe, once again, what a lovely home she had at her young age while he, close to a decade her senior, made only a police inspector's salary and probably had a crappy one-room apartment in the squalid Tenderloin district.

"In the short time I've known you," he was saying, "you seem convinced that men are attracted to you only because you are a public figure and that they think they have something to gain by knowing you. I merely wanted to show you how it really is."

"Well, you don't know shit." There was nothing that enraged her more than losing an argument—and she sure as hell wasn't *winning* this one. She especially didn't like it that her opponent was a big, handsome man who was sitting back on her oversized sofa, wearing a goofy smile as if he'd had too much to drink.

"Don't I? Here is what I *do* know that maybe you *don't*, even if I've already told you. Some guy out there is after you. Why, I don't know. Maybe you knew him way back when and he still figures he has a score to settle with you. Or maybe, as he's indicated, you rejected his friend and he's out to get you for *that.*" He paused. "Desirée, people jump off bridges or shoot themselves over being dumped by the ones they adore. Passion is a scary thing. People are scary animals."

"Well, he's got me confused with someone else. I haven't broken any hearts lately."

"What about before you moved here? Boston, Chicago—"

She shook her head. "No broken hearts there, either."

Harris had just experienced the overwhelming force of Desirée's lust. She didn't know her powers. He thought for a moment about unlikely it was that any man could be intimate with her and just put aside and get on with life.

"There's no jilted boyfriend or his buddy trying to snuff me out," she drawled as she stared at her blank, 42-inch TV screen. "No dates here. Got too much stuff to do without worrying about getting prettied up for some guy who's probably a closet queen anyway."

"Don't be so damn flippant. I need information."

She wheeled around and said, her eyes blazing, "Just give it up, OK?"

"Can't do that," he said with the seriousness of a trial lawyer. "It's a criminal case. Got a potential stalker who's making threatening calls to a radio talk-show host." They stared at each other for several long moments and he added, "Maybe no one here in the Bay Area, but like I said, where else? You've moved around a lot, worked at a handful of stations. You've done live appearances, shaken hands and so on. Anyone in those cities ever had the nerve to hit on you, ask you out?"

"Just you," she deadpanned.

"I have the right to remain silent. Anything I say will be used against me in a court of law..."

They both laughed for a moment. She wandered

over to the front window, which looked out onto Juanita Way. She pulled the drapes slightly apart and gazed out, as Harris had often seen her do. She did some of her best thinking in front of windows.

"What you're asking," Desirée said, "is how many enemies I have. You've heard me on the radio. You know what I do—I provoke the public. Everyone on the air at KCA is a potential victim for harassment just by doing their job. It's sort of an occupational hazard."

Harris pondered this. "OK. At the station, have you made any enemies?"

"At KCA, we all treat each other with courtesy and impartiality. Everyone is a nice professional. Everyone is a professional nice."

"Everyone?"

"Yep. Kelvin Barrow, Ernie Ford, Jay Otari..."

"What about the boy who needs a haircut? The intern."

Her eyes narrowed. "Matt?"

"Yeah. He's got the hots for you real bad. He would give anything to be with you here right now, doing what we did a few minutes ago."

She blushed. "Don't say that. Matt? Horny for *me?* I'm getting some disturbing images in my head. Now I know why I've been calling you Dirty Harry. It's your *mind."* She then waved him over, suddenly serious, "I want you to see something."

He joined her and looked out at the dark, deserted, car-lined street. She said, "That man...across the street. Are those binoculars? *He's watching me."*

"Move," Harris instructed, pulling her away from the window. "Stay here until I get back." She nodded as she watched him reach into his sportscoat and take out his service weapon. The night's levity was over. Dirty Harry, kidder and kisser minutes earlier, all pumped up now and ready for action, opened the front door and hustled down the stairs. Business as usual. She locked her front door, closed her drapes and, knowing that it would be pointless to force herself to watch TV, went to bed.

Outside, Harris scarcely noticed the chill San Francisco wind blowing through his hair as he hurried across the street, gun in hand, and searched for the man Desirée had seen. Most of the houses on Juanita Way were like Desirée's: big, elegant, plaster Victorians, dark now, their smug, complacent, successful young occupants now asleep, the streets lined with fashionable imported cars—some of which would be stolen probably by year's end—the whole neighborhood now deserted and peaceful in a way unimaginable during daylight hours.

He was sure Desirée had seen someone, although he wasn't convinced that the man had been the caller. Probably, it was just some straggler who stared with envy at the young woman standing in the fancy living room. Embarrassed at being seen, the man had hurried away. Well, Harris thought, there was no law against walking the streets or staring at a woman in her living room.

Back at her house's front door, he called her on his cell phone. "It's me. I couldn't find anyone."

Back inside, he said, "It's best not to take these things too seriously. But always keep your drapes closed at night."

"Maybe I should just move back to freakin' Louisiana." Desirée sat down and lit a cigarette as her hands shook.

"Don't get excited," Harris said.

"'Excited'? I'm a little bit past that point, fella. If that guy out there was the caller, it means he knows where I work and live." She blew out a huge stream of smoke. "Maybe I should ask Kelvin if Monique and I can move into the radio station. Or if I could do my show from my bedroom. Those are the only two places where I would feel safe."

"Maybe you should take a leave of absence...?"

"Not an option. I just have to keep going as I have been." She got up suddenly and started pacing again. Presently she said, "You don't have to stay here all night, you know. That sofa isn't as comfortable as it looks. But if you want to do it, go ahead. I'm off to bed."

...

The man was tired but satisfied as he arrived home just before dawn. After walking by her house and being seen by that bastard cop, he's had to hurry back to his car. But he'd gotten away, although the cop could have caught him if he'd tried. It had taken the man most of the night of driving aimlessly through the Bay Area before his pulse settled down. He didn't like that kind of excitement; he liked it when things went according to plan.

At home, he showered and changed out of his dark clothes. Then he ate leftovers, turned on his TV and stared at CNN's pretty blonde anchor with the sound off. But he couldn't concentrate on her. He couldn't think about anything except what he had done that night.

So *that's* where the cunt lives, he thought, picturing the fine white Juanita Way house. The man didn't live in such a nice place. His one-bedroom apartment, judging by its smell, had probably been home to hundreds of chain-smoking, flatulent men over the years. But he liked where he lived. It was funky and squalid, yes, but the neighbors were as indifferent to him as he was to them, and the cops hated going near such places.

He looked over at his picture of Michael, whose frozen smile reminded him of all the big plans they had made together, all the great things they were going to do in the years ahead.

But things didn't turn out that way. Sometimes things just went bad and you couldn't help it. But other times you could find the person who was to blame—or at least partly to blame—and make them pay.

The cunt would pay. How many times had he said those very words to Michael's picture? Michael had only smiled. Well, soon Michael would have reason to smile.

The man had reason to smile, too. He had found out things recently about computers and hacking. The information was there if you wanted to learn it, and he had learned plenty. He had gotten into a Website or two and found just about everything a fella might want to know about a certain Desirée Justine Dupree. Her home address and phone number, her sister's name. Probably could have found out when they had their periods, for God's sake.

The time was coming soon. When it was over, if he survived, he would figure out what to do next, where to go. But for now he had his work waiting for him. He picked up the phone and started doing what he did best.

...

Monique bounded out of her bedroom in an oversized white T-shirt that bore the horribly faded image of the rock band U2. She walked down the hallway, quizzing herself on what was likely to be on that morning's midterm examination. She felt sure she would get through the test easily—she usually did—but believed it never hurt to be overprepared.

She was scratching her scalp, as she always did in the mornings, and wasn't looking where she was going as she headed into the kitchen for her first cup of coffee of the day and slammed into Harris.

"Hey—!" She immediately stopped scratching her scalp and suddenly felt deeply embarrassed about her style of dress.

"Mornin', Monique," Harris muttered with a pasted-on smile.

She eyed him. "Did you spend the night here?"

He nodded. "But relax. I spent the night on the sofa. I was just protecting the Dupree women."

"On the sofa? It's big, but you're bigger. A *lot* bigger."

"Tell me about it. Worst night I've spent in a long time."

"You spent the whole night on our sofa to protect us?" Monique said. "No kidding?"

He looked at her levelly. "I never kid."

She nodded. "I like that in a cop."

What else do you like? he wanted to ask. But he had just told her he wasn't a kidder, so he let the remark go unspoken. "Let's have some coffee," he said.

He didn't want coffee, really. He wanted to go home and crash for twelve hours. But that wasn't an option just yet. He had to find out who was harassing Desirée. Then he could hibernate. But Desirée came first, and it was damn important that he get the caller before the caller got to her. And it looked as though the guy was getting closer. The guy wasn't a moron, either. He was a systematic, methodical urban terrorist.

Just then the telephone rang. Monique picked it up, Harris gestured to hand it to him, and she did. Desirée had already answered. Harris listened, putting on his most inscrutable face for Monique, who, he could see, assumed immediately—and correctly—who was on the line.

Soon, Harris hung up the phone, took out his cell phone and made a call. "Get him?" he asked, then sighed.

"We just have that phone disconnected," Monique said, her face full of concern, her T-shirt sweated through at the armpits.

"Yeah. I don't think he has your cell numbers."

"Not yet, anyway."

"He won't. We're getting closer. I better go talk to Desirée about this."

"When will this nightmare end?" she asked, almost pleading.

Damned if I know, Harris thought. "Soon. Goddamn soon. I promise."

He went down the hallway to her bedroom and

found her staring out the window. Her bedroom was not unlike his own: neutral in style, no frills, practical. The bedroom of someone with more important things to do than decorate. He sat on the bed, inches from her, and stared out the window too.

"That was him just now. That was him last night," she said in a thin, despairing voice. He could see her practically vibrate with anxiety.

"He's getting brazen. He's getting cocky. When they think they can just walk up to your home, they get sloppy and we catch 'em."

She let out a harsh, bitter laugh. "You had your chance last fucking night, Dirty Harry. He stood right outside my building and you let him get away."

Harris's face darkened. "Don't play into his hand. He wants you to have a nervous breakdown and kill yourself, to spare him the trouble. Just stay tough and let Anchor and me catch this guy. Hear me?"

She eyed him. "You'll only be here a short while."

"Oh? Says who?"

She arched her back and scratched her face. She stared at her legs, which were pasty and sweaty. "I don't think I can walk. I'm afraid that if I get up, my legs will give out and I'll just fall through to the center of the earth."

Harris pulled back her hair. "Do as the song says," he whispered. "'Lean on me.'"

He pulled her into his arms, amazed at the childlike narrowness of her, the utter surrender. He had subdued violent suspects in such a manner, immobilizing their flailing limbs with the most awkward, intimate of embraces.

"Don't worry," he murmured. "Nothing's gonna happen." But his mind raced back to jumpy images of Juanita Way at night, underlit and unpopulated but for a figure all in black. Harris knew he couldn't have caught him in a foot race; the man had too much of a lead. Plus, drawing his weapon and shooting the man, if the man had been doing nothing more than standing on the sidewalk, would have cost Harris his career. Maybe more.

He sighed. "OK now? Ready to face the world?"

She nodded. "Yeah." Then, "Didn't know you were capable of such empathy, Cavanaugh."

"I'm not. I'm an amoral, fascist pig, Dupree, and don't you forget it."

She snuffled and wiped her nose. "Next time I'm on the air ragging on the San Francisco police, I'll be sure to mention your name."

They rose together and headed out to the kitchen. Monique was making breakfast. "Want some?"

Harris wasn't sure if Monique meant breakfast or something else. Yes, he wanted whatever she was prepared to provide. "Hope there's enough for three," he said.

"Oh, Desirée never eats breakfast," Monique said.

"It's about time she started," said Harris.

Desirée spun around, frowning. "Hey, Dirty Harry—"

"And after you eat, take a shower and shampoo your hair. You're getting pretty funky, you know."

Desirée marched out of the kitchen and headed for the bathroom. As he heard the bathroom door close, he said to Monique, "How come she didn't tell me she was divorced?"

"I suppose because you didn't ask."

He pointed at her. "How come *you* didn't tell me?"

"Same answer."

"So: could it be that the ex is somehow involved in all this?"

She shrugged. "They haven't seen each other in years. I seriously doubt that he knows she's out here in the Bay Area."

"Were they still on reasonably good terms during the divorce?" he asked.

"Well, they *did* call it quits. But there were no fistfights, so far as I know."

Monique would make a good doctor when medical school was over, Harris thought. She already understood people and life far better than most people her age.

"Hard to imagine anyone divorcing Desirée," Harris said, then immediately regretted how it sounded. But then he realized that Monique already sensed the depth of his interest in Desirée. It was hard to put anything past the Dupree women.

"It was an efficient divorce and Desirée has never really said anything about it," Monique explained. "So I've never asked. Still, if you must know, *he* initiated the proceedings."

"Any ideas on why that happened?"

"Oh, I think it may have had something to do with the fact that he had fallen deeply in love with some other man's wife. The two lovebirds left their mates and flew off together." Then, "I hope you aren't going to tell Desirée that I ratted her out like this."

"You aren't ratting," he told her. "You're giving me information I need for my investigation."

"Desirée and Rob were doomed from the start. Our parents died shortly after the wedding. She was becoming the radio personality she is today—if you know what I mean—and he was trying to get his candidate elected to the Louisiana state legislature. It didn't take the candidate and many others long to figure out that Rob was married to the Mouth of the South."

"I think I'm beginning to understand," Harris said.

She stood above him and sipped her coffee. "Desirée wasn't about to cool it on the air and Rob was under a lot of pressure to shut her up, and our parents had died and I came to live with them. Not a happy situation."

"I guess not."

Harris pictured the French Quarter of New Orleans, an unconventionally pretty, headstrong young woman trying to cope with a huge personal loss while making significant professional gains. An ambitious young man, married to this woman, afraid for his own professional future, insisting that she stop being herself in order to please him. Then her sister moves in, a teenaged beauty. It was almost too much to believe. "He sounds like a jerk. Maybe it was for the best that they split."

"I thought so. I thought he was a creep from day one."

"Well, why did she marry that clown, anyway?" he asked.

"He wasn't as bad as all that," said Desirée, drying her hair in the doorway.

# CHAPTER 5

Desirée had pulled back her hair and put on a white terrycloth bathrobe which was a major improvement over the faded orange Giants jersey she had slept in. Harris thought at once that she should always wear whites and pastels instead of the garish clothes he usually saw her in. She glowered at him as she entered the kitchen.

"Dez." Monique tried to sound diplomatic.

"Yes. I'm Dez. You're Monique and he's nosy."

"It all seemed relevant," Monique said. "He needed to know some things."

"So you told him. And now he knows. So why don't you head on out to school now?"

Harris had heard this tone in her voice on the air. Even Bette Davis couldn't sound bitchier. Monique heard it, too. She slipped into her bedroom, changed quickly and was gone.

"Now," Desirée said to Harris. "Want to know about *me*, ask me, not my goddamn sister. Understand?"

"I'm a cop. I have a job to do. If Person A won't give me the information, I ask Person B. If I tiptoed around and was afraid to offend people by asking questions, I would never solve a case."

"Apparently you didn't hear what I just said——"

"And apparently you didn't hear me, either. Why don't you just sit your ass down and have some breakfast? It'll put you into a better frame of mind."

The kitchen was filled with the fresh smells of eggs, bacon, toast and coffee. Desirée weakened and filled her plate, then sat down and shoveled forkfuls into her mouth. "Just mind your own business," she muttered after swallowing. "That was ancient history and a very difficult time in her life. She doesn't need to be reminded of it."

"She's a gorgeous young woman thriving in medical school who has more boyfriends than she can count," Harris said. "I don't exactly look at her and think, 'Poor baby.'"

Desirée stared at him, the same way she stared at callers who made points she couldn't refute. "You heard me. Just watch your step and don't start pelting my sister with questions."

He stared back. "I'm going to get valid information from the available sources." Then, "How would you like it if one Robert La Porte, your ex, was the caller and we were delayed in arresting him because you wouldn't cooperate?"

Desirée rolled her eyeballs. "I can assure you he ain't your guy." She ate another bite of breakfast and took several sips of coffee. "I married him because I was young and dumb and he had success written all over him. But then, as my sister explained, I had this radio show to do and I was, uh, politically outspoken and my hubby's people pressured him to tell me to shut up. And along the way he met someone else who was much more the kind of woman who would obey him." She paused. "A lot of gays and lesbians call me on the air about gay marriage. I want to tell them to forget about marriage. Just shack up for the rest of your lives, or till you get tired of each other. Then you can call it quits." She added, "Do you know what the leading cause of divorce is?"

"What is it?"

"Marriage."

He smirked. "I guess I sort of stepped right into that one."

"Remember, you're having breakfast with the Ragin' Cajun."

"So you got divorced. Then what?"

"It's all a blur. I was making it in New Orleans talk radio. Monique was living with me. The Big Easy got too small for me so I sent out demo tapes and got a bite from Chicago for a lot more money, so up we went. Have you ever lived through a Great Lakes winter? Jesus! Then Boston, where the weather was almost as bad. KCA made me an offer I couldn't refuse, so we moved here. I did my radio show, Monique went to school. She did her thing, I did mine. We've put everything else behind us."

"So your ex didn't threaten you?"

"No, he wasn't that kind of guy. He met someone else and I suppose they'll live happily ever after. He was as goal-oriented as I was, so I don't guess that a little thing like a divorce would devastate him."

"People sometimes do the thing we least expect them to do. Remember Ted Bundy? Handsome, charming young man, right? Those young women he dated let him into their apartments because they didn't think he was a sociopath."

Desirée tucked away some more breakfast. "My ex wasn't sociopathic. He was indifferent, though. He used people in a nice way, while I have no use for that sort of manipulative, exploitative bullshit. Just a chapter in someone's life, that's all it was."

"For just a chapter, you seem to remember it very,

very vividly," Harris said.

"Well, maybe it was more than that. After all, I *was* married to the guy. You should Google him and see what comes up. I haven't heard a word from him in years."

She finished her breakfast as Harris grinned at how much of a breakfast person she was despite her refusal at first to eat.

"So," she asked, "is this part of your job?"

"Is what part of my job?"

"Spending the night here. Having breakfast with me. Holding me while I cry."

"Some of it is," he said. "The rest is at my own discretion."

She made a face. "I won't ask which is which."

"I appreciate that."

"San Francisco, like Boston, has no discernable seasons," Desirée observed. "We're coming up to spring break, and yet you'd never know it just by looking out the window."

"Well, at least be grateful there's no snow here, either. Or if there is, it lasts about twenty seconds."

"Oh, I'm not complaining. I was just thinking that Monique should go somewhere, to get away from all this craziness I'm having to deal with right now."

"Maybe the two of you should go to where the sun is." He appraised her as he drank his coffee. "Online you can get a decent deal—or a bad one—on airfare to Mexico."

"I can't take time off work. It's my problem, not hers." She sighed. "After seeing him on the street and then you took off after him...and the call a few minutes ago...it seemed like the only thing to do was run. But that goes contrary to my nature. I didn't bust my ass for a decade for this job just to get run out of town by some deranged guy out there." Then, "My terror is mixed with curiosity. Who is he and why does he have it in for me? Frankly, I'm dying to find out what this is really all about."

"You and me both," said Harris.

"So no more bullshit from me. You ask, I answer."

He arched his eyebrows. "No bullshit?"

"None." She rested her hand on her chin. "I've seen you look better, Dirty Harry. Difficult time sleeping on my oversized sofa?"

"It was awful. But you look pretty sexy."

"Didn't you say I was all funky and needed a shower?"

"Well, you did. And I hate that damn Giants thing you sleep in. But now you're fresh, bright and scrubbed. You're just about the cutest Southern belle around."

"Oh, you're just saying that because I let you spend the night."

"Seriously, a little later on I want to talk to you

about us," he said.

"I didn't know there was an 'us.'"

"Well, we sort of do. You know how I feel about you. I know how you feel about me. We have to deal with those issues."

Desirée shrugged, not knowing what top say and eager to change the subject and never return to this one. What did he mean about knowing how she felt about him? She still hadn't sorted out her feelings for him, though she knew she had them.

"It's a shame we didn't meet in another time and place," he was saying. "But that's how it is. If you start to feel that our relationship, whatever it is, is inappropriate, I can arranged to have myself replaced."

"So far, we're OK," she said.

. . .

Desirée appeared before him in a white dress that nearly caused him to drop his coffee cup. She usually dressed in ways that didn't make him notice how sexy and dark her French complexion was, and if there was something he had a weakness for, it was a dark woman in a white dress.

"Like it?" she asked. "It's sort of my Audrey Hepburn look."

"Nice," he said, unable to say more. Audrey Hepburn never looked so good. Her reddish hair tumbled over her shoulders in a most exotic, alluring fashion.

She had a personal appearance to make at the station that afternoon. It wouldn't do to have her speaking to the public in her usual attire. "OK if we put on the radio?" she asked as he turned on the car's ignition.

"Only if it's not your station."

"Haha."

On KCA, the late-morning duo was interviewing the latest New York *Times* reporter to write a book on the war in Iraq. At the break, they reminded their audience that Desirée Dupree would be making an appearance that afternoon.

"More goddamn commercials on this station," Harris said as he and Desirée were bombarded with a two-minute spot on some high-powered, portable AM/FM radio that was supposed to be just the thing when an earthquake knocked out all other communication systems. Then another sixty seconds about that Union Square jewelry store that had been around forever. Then a commercial about an appliance store in Daly City that had been around even longer than the Union Square jewelry store.

"That's what you get when Arbitron says you've been number one in the Bay Area for the past twenty-five ratings periods," Desirée said.

"What's their secret?" Harris asked. He *knew* their secret: charismatic, obnoxious air personalities like Desirée Dupree, the Ragin' Cajun. Plus, the station had a powerful signal. You could hear it in Canada and Mexico.

"Brutal, ruthless management. Kelvin is the nicest

guy in the world, but if your ratings fall, he'll boot your fanny out the door. And it'll take him about five seconds to find your replacement."

"You're in no imminent danger," he said. "The masses listen in every night you're on, despite all those insipid commercials."

"Yep, I'm one they love to hate." She laughed.

Or the one they hate to love, Harris thought. And love her they did. Her ratings were nearly double those of her competitors, some of whom might indirectly lose their jobs because of their inability to keep up with Desirée. Could those people be possible menacing callers, or somehow be behind all the ugliness? He doubted it. He had run a check on everyone in the industry and found nothing. Keep searching, he told himself. The guy is out there and won't go away.

Desirée gazed out the window, admiring the surprisingly sunny day. A brisk breeze blew through the trees. Sutro Tower stood in the distance. The fog would probably start to blow in, too. The hills were everywhere. So were the cars, parked in the oddest ways on the hills. San Francisco in some ways reminded her of Boston, with its compact size and cool climate. But both cities mostly just convinced her that she was a Dixie chick from the Big Easy. Once a Southerner, always a Southerner. She let her mind wander back to the South for a moment and wondered if she would ever return there permanently. Monique probably wouldn't—she was beautiful and smart and was doing just fine in San Francisco. She would graduate, practice, marry one of the guys who worshiped her and live happily ever after.

"Earth calling Desirée," Harris said.

"Yes?"

"We've arrived."

"This isn't the radio station," she said. "Looks like Russian Hill." She peered out through the top of the windshield. "Yeah, there's Alcatraz, all right."

"This is Taylor Street, to be precise." He pointed

to what once obviously had been a mansion. It was now converted into beige condos, like most of the other residences in this neighborhood. "That's my home."

They climbed out of his car and went inside. The lobby was wide but quaint. It smelled of wood polish and wool. Desirée had seen any number of movies set in San Francisco where the apartment lobbies looked just like this one. "How much rent do you pay?"

"No rent. I own it."

"No mortgage?"

"Nope."

"Who died and left you a million dollars?"

"Nobody died. They're still around. They've got theirs, I've got mine." He paused. "I've been here all my life. In fact, my family came here around the Gold Rush of Eighteen-fifty. You live in the same place for that long, you're bound to make some progress."

"So you were a member of the lucky sperm club," she said. "Then why aren't you doing something really lucrative? Or just roaming around the world, spending your money?"

"Because I didn't think I was cut out for the life of a spoiled brat." Then, "I'll share something with you. I have a friend who used to manage accounts for IBM in the Financial District. She was making six figures a year, working her butt off and hating every minute of it. So she quit. Want to know what she's doing now? She sits at Fisherman's Wharf with a box of colored chalk, making portraits of tourists. She barely makes enough to live on but the work is a *lot* more fun than anything she ever did for Big Blue. I think there's a lesson to be learned in her story."

"Well, if she's happy, I'm happy for her," Desirée said. "You better get showered. We have to be there a few minutes early so I can go over some technical things with them."

"Yeah. Just make yourself at home while I do my thing."

He disappeared into the bathroom and she sat on a leather sofa. Lighting up a cigarette, she laughed, looking around. The place had to be two thousand sqaure feet, with an eagle's-eye view of Alcatraz Island and the Golden Gate Bridge. Hardwood floors, leather furniture and a Sony high-definition TV as big as hers. So the cop's family had money. She thought she knew the names of San Francisco's most prominent families: Crocker, Stanford, Huntington, Hopkins. Add Cavanaugh to the list. Harris owned a Russian Hill condo and worked as a cop for the enjoyment of it. She blushed, flashing back to her first meeting with him at the radio station. How she had regarded him and his partner, Anchor, with such naked condescension. How she had paced about the living room of her house, thinking that he couldn't possibly ever have been in anything as delightful as her home and surely envied her brains and talent! In truth, she was mortgaged up to the eyeballs, and her place was worth maybe half as much as his Russian Hill condo.

Well, now, she was getting to know him just a

little bit better, and she was getting just a little bit humbler. She stubbed out her cigarette, walked across the room and gazed out the window.

Who *was* Desirée Justine Dupree? Only some Dixie hick who had played the game and gotten lucky. She was popular *now*, but what about next year? Radio, as much as TV or the movies, was a fickle business. Kelvin wouldn't hesitate to fire her if her broad audience grew bored with her rap and tuned in to hear someone else's.

She didn't want to be there in Harris's home. She just wanted him to catch the guy who was responsible for her misery so she could go back to work and forget about her troubles. Or at least forget about her troubles with the mystery caller and simply deal with the normal troubles of everyday life.

"Desirée?" He emerged from the bathroom.

She turned to face him. "Yes?"

"Just this." He grabbed and kissed her.

She pulled away. "No. This is wrong."

"Who says?"

"It just is." She blinked, as if clearing her mind as well as her eyes, remembering where she was and why he was in her life. "You're taking advantage."

"You weren't exactly fighting me off." Then, "You should spend the night here."

She wiped her mouth, as if trying to wipe away the memory of his kiss. "No. Let's just leave and pretend this didn't happen."

"Why? I don't imagine there's anyone else in your life."

"Nobody else," she said. "Just me and my neuroses."

"And how do we overcome your neuroses?"

"*We* don't," she said. "*I* live with them. What obsesses me right now is the possibility of waking up some night and having this mysterious caller standing over me naked with his dick in one hand and a switchblade in the other."

He chuckled.

She said, "I'm rejecting you because you're a cop."

"Well, what of it?"

"My father carried a badge, too. I'll tell you all about it sometime. But not today. Especially not right now, just before I have to be pumped up for a live appearance. And I need you to give me my breathing room and forget about getting it on with me. If that's what you *really* want, just go check out the strippers at the O'Farrell Theatre and jerk yourself off." She stared at him. "I have things to do today. Ready to go?"

He nodded. "Ready. And we'll talk about only those things you want. Or not talk at all. Today, *you're* the boss."

# CHAPTER 6

"Damn, this is *huge*," Harris said as they stood inside the front entrance of Cyber City. The superstore carried computers and a hundred other things—or a thousand. Everywhere, big plastic overhead signs read COMPUTERS, CELL PHONES, PERSONAL AUDIO, CAR AUDIO, MAJOR APPLIANCES, DVD'S. "It's like a warehouse. In fact, it probably *was* a warehouse."

"There are two Cyber City stores just like this one in the East Bay," Desirée said, "and probably lots more nationwide. They're all as big as this one. That's why it's way out here in the boonies, where land is cheaper. Could you imagine something this big on Market Street?"

Desirée had agreed to greet the customers for a few hours and read a list of the store's specials on the air a few times. An easy afternoon.

"Well," she added, browsing through a brochure, "at least Cyber City is what it claims to be."

"And what does it claim to be?" Harris asked.

"Sort of a Wal-Mart. This place carries all this stock and marks it way down and because they've got such a huge volume of merchandise. They still make money."

"Everybody wins," Harris said.

"Not at all," Desirée told him. "All these inexpensive new gadgets will become obsolete before you know it. The cell phones will crap out. The computers' software will become dated. When you look at it that way, this stuff really isn't such a bargain after all."

Harris gaped again at the stunning display of merchandise. A colossal sign against a wall listed the manufacturers of some of Cyber City's wares:

SONY, TOSHIBA, PANASONIC, IBM, HEWLETT-PACKARD, COMPAQ, APPLE. "Whew! Do we really *need* all this stuff?"

Desirée smirked. "Don't need it. Just *want* it."

"Oh."

They didn't say much to each other after that. Harris gave Desirée her space but stayed nearby, discreetly screening the customers who, seeing the KCA banner and remote equipment, came close enough to discern that the swarthy, pretty blonde with the microphone was the barracuda who ate callers alive.

Afterwards, Harris drove Desirée back to her house with just a curt "See ya"; later, Desirée did her show while Christina sat in a corner of the studio by the huge window, pushing buttons on her handheld electronic crossword puzzle, oblivious to the sparkling San Francisco Bay behind her. She prided herself on being able to assimilate quickly to every situation—she knew how to get busy and how to relax. Desirée, she could see, had two states: tense and tenser. The woman needed to read a few books on relaxation and decompression.

At the moment, Desirée was garrulous, silencing her callers with the mute button. The miracle of Desirée Dupree, Christina concluded, was that she didn't *sound* nervous at all despite looking pale and cold with fear and panic. Christina had heard stories about Johnny Carson—in real life, he was as shy as a three-year-old and reclusive as a hermit. But on the set of *The Tonight Show* he became the most urbane and charming of men when the camera's red light flashed on. In a downtown San Francisco hotel, Christina had shared an elevator ride with the actor Richard Gere and found him plump and plain; but on any big screen or magazine cover he was svelte and handsome. The camera loved Carson and Gere, just as the microphone adored Desirée.

To Christina, Desirée's low, faintly Southern voice and abrasive candor lent her a sort of slummy sexiness that made Christina picture her as the charming, well-spoken barmaid in a Tenderloin beer joint, explaining the world to a handful of boozing losers. That maybe explained her appeal to some of her listeners. It was easy to feel superior to Desirée Dupree, with her anger, idealism and bumpkin twang. But even if you didn't like her and considered yourself her intellectual superior, you just somehow felt compelled to listen to her five nights a week.

"Just between you and me, Chuck," Desirée was saying to the caller from San Leandro as much of the Bay Area listened, "the major politicians of the Democratic and Republican parties don't have a dime's worth of difference between them. Conservatives yearn for political power. Liberals yearn for political power. The status quo exists because the people with the power to change things want to keep everything as it is."

Amen to that, Christina thought. Then she wondered: Doesn't the station's management worry when Desirée so brazenly criticizes the establishment? Probably not, as long as she was just sounding off. If she told people to *do* something—to stop paying taxes or challenge the establishment in some other practical, illegal way...well, *that* would upset the suits upstairs at Broadcast House.

Desirée went to a break. She looked over her shoulder at Christina and said, "I'm going to get some coffee. Want some?"

"I thought the intern kid did those things."

"I think he's done for the night."

"Want me to go get it?"

"No," Desirée said, "I need the exercise." She hurried out of the studio and padded down the hallway to the kitchen, the ubiquitous commercials, spilling from ceiling speakers, trailing her like relentless salesmen. The kitchen lights had ceased their erratic flicker; Jimmy, she surmised, must have finally fixed them. She got two white ceramic mugs and was about to fill them when she saw the silhouette of a man about to plunge a knife into her.

With a guttural cry of terror she flung the mugs at the darkened male shape.

The silhouetted figure emerged. Jimmy. His knife

was actually a screwdriver. He replaced it in his toolbelt and said, "Miz Dupree! You all right?"

She clutched her heaving chest, her eyes bulging and watery. "Oh, Jimmy!"

Christina burst in, her gun drawn. Jimmy shouted, "The police! Look out!" He dived at Desirée's feet, avoiding the anticipated spray of bullets.

Desirée shrugged at Christina. "No harm done, Inspector. A simple misunderstanding. I thought it was just you, me and Jay in here tonight."

"I'm on my way out. Just got done changin' all the burned-out lightbulbs," said Jimmy, slowly struggling to his feet with Desirée's unsolicited assistance. "Broadcast House is a new place, but things burn out real fast around here. Sure sucks up a lot of electricity, this joint." He shook his head in gentle derision of modern technology.

Desirée listened for a moment. The familiar arrangement of commercials. Her break was far from over. She wished to be away from these people and this situation. "I better get on back in there and earn my keep."

Jimmy, his face broadening into an idiot's grin, said, "Go get 'em, girl!"

Back in the studio she sat back in her swivel chair and listened with distracted shame as the commercials ran, shaking her head at herself for going berserk over aging electricians working overtime. Presently Christina came in with two steaming mugs of coffee and set one down in front of Desirée.

"Sorry about what happened in the kitchen."

Christina shook her head the tiniest bit. "Don't be. It broke up my night. Good thing I didn't blow him away."

Desirée held her profusely steaming mug under her nose, appreciating the coffee's freshness. "This must be pretty boring for you. Radio is not a spectator sport."

Christina smiled. "I've had worse assignments."

Desirée swiveled around to face the other woman and at that instant realized what she wanted at that particular stage in her life. Friendship, camaraderie, girl talk, for which her sister was inadequate. Monique, engrossed in medical school at U.C.S.F., came and went with revolving-door frequency and, probably inadvertently, already had become the center of a clique of classmates. She was several years younger than Desirée and never, in Desirée's mind, remotely a peer.

Although Monique would have vehemently denied it, Desirée had grown convinced that the younger woman regarded her sister and breadwinner with the gentlest, friendliest condescension because Desirée had not attended college and earned her living—and Monique's—at a job that Monique probably thought of as unskilled labor. Monique had never been to Desirée's workplace, had no exact idea of where Broadcast House and listened to the Ragin' Cajun only when she felt like it. Desirée, at her lowest, most self-pitying moments, saw herself as essentially friendless in the world.

"Tell me," she asked Christina Anchor, "why did you choose police work?"

Christina thought for a moment. "I suppose it looked exciting. I couldn't have endured a nine-to-five grind behind a desk. And I sure couldn't have done the nerve-wracking work *you* do. What if they stop calling or listening...?"

"*Never!*" Desirée chuckled. "I offend them too much for that to happen." She glanced at the bare fingers on Christina's left hand. "Why aren't you married?"

Christina's forehead furrowed into frown. *What's it to ya?* But then her face softened and she looked in Desirée's direction. "Some men aren't interested in a woman with a gun. It's just too phallic for them. I hope you didn't get the idea that I had some sort of personal relationship with Harris."

"Well..."

She cleared her throat. "Sorry to disappoint you. Sometimes people think that a woman and a man can't work together without playing slap-and-tickle."

"It *had* crossed my mind." Desirée at first had thought Anchor and Cavanaugh could have starred in a cop show called *Tough and Good-looking*. She imagined relentless, unresolved sexual tension between the two and wondered how it could have gone unconsummated. She also fantasized about carnal opportunities between herself and Harris, but then realized that she had no more chance of such an encounter than a man drooling over *Playboy* magazine could step into the vivid pictures and ravish the featured models.

"People probably have wondered the same thing about you at your age," Christina said. "You're the youngest woman on the air here. Great job, big money. Was there a casting couch involved...?"

"This is just radio, darlin'," Desirée drawled, "and just local radio. I'm no Doctor Laura or Kim Commando. And I'm certainly no Oprah. TV and the movies are where the *really* big money is. My boss doesn't want to ball me. He just wants high ratings.

If mine fall, I'm history. But for now, I'm here and I like my job and that's enough."

Christina nodded. "Job satisfaction is the main thing." After a minute or so, she added, "Harris seems to thrive on the dangers of his job. He made the right career choice."

"He's the kind of man I could see myself with," Desirée confided. Her mind wandered for a moment to the commercials murmuring overhead: animated voices, urgent music, empty promises.

"He's not here for that. A personal relationship with you. I'm sure he would consider that unethical."

Desirée shrugged. "It won't happen. It doesn't matter, anyway. I would be happy just with stability right now."

"Stability is boring," said Christina. "You want more."

Desirée smiled. "Right now, boring old stability would be good enough."

They fell silent for a long moment. Christina, sipping her coffee, looked past Desirée at the microphone that resembled a huge dark fuzzy phallus and the blinking lights of the telephone. She hated Broadcast House. Each time she entered the granite-floored, oak-paneled building, her stomach fluttered with anxiety, as if, upstairs in the KCA studio, the Ragin' Cajun awaited to grill her on the air as to why she and Dirty Harry had as yet failed to identify, much less apprehend, the harassing caller.

While poking at her digital crossword-puzzle game Christina listened sometimes to Desirée's mellifluous voice in on-air debates and relived, briefly and reluctantly, the handful of occasions she herself had attempted public speaking, during a play in high school and sometimes in front of her colleagues at the police station. She, in her own opinion, had performed adequately—after all, she had simply read what was in front of her—but invariably left the podium or lectern terrified and intimidated, her throat parched and armpits flooded.

Once, when Christina was a teenager, a boyfriend had taken her to a Linda Ronstadt concert at the Oakland Coliseum. Their seats, front-row center, were within half a Frisbee's throw of the stage. Christina watched, with an awe she had scarcely expected to feel, as Ronstadt sashayed onstage to an explosion of cheers and applause. Flashbulbs popped white light like myriad strobe lights.

Resplendent in a lovely white-silk dress, her hair tumbling to her shoulders in shellacked waves, the singer greeted the crowd with an impossibly bright, mirthful smile and the heartiest of waves, her brown eyes as big and round as Mexican moons. The band exuberantly played the songs that seemed to comprise the California soundtrack of the 1970s. Ronstadt crooned, clutching the microphone, hips subtly swaying and eyes often shut tightly.

Christina, clinging onto her boyfriend's arm as they left the Coliseum after the third or fourth encore, became Linda Ronstadt's newest admirer, if not precisely her fan—the girl would never have spent her own money to see the singer perform, and was as likely as not to turn off Ronstadt's music as it played on the radio. But Christina had the deepest respect for talent and courage and knew that, besides inherent vocal ability, Ronstadt had something special which enabled her to perform before thousands—what could one call it? Poise, élan, panache? Christina Anchor knew she herself would be incapable of cultivating such a quality in a dozen lifetimes.

This Ronstadt memory returned to her as she sat near Desirée, listening to the radio host's low-toned, flawless oratory delivered to masses unseen. Desirée's was definitely not a show-business voice, devoid of flimflam and coming from someplace other than than her sinuses—her throat, to be exact, and with a warm and womanly intonation. Were Desirée, just for fun, to insist that Christina slide up to the microphone for a brief, spontaneous interview, the cop feared becoming as incapacitated by panic as if, on that balmy Oakland evening in the 1970s, Linda Ronstadt had pulled her up onstage to sing along and shake a tambourine.

Christina blinked away such disturbing, pointless thoughts and turned to Desirée. "You're coping well." Desirée nodded, wincing at the idiocy of the commercial running at that moment.

"For now." She paused, as if considering Christina's remark not much more intelligent than the muted commercial.

"Not running scared, I mean. You know we'll catch him. Right?"

"Right." Desirée pointed to the multi-line telephone system. "We're all lit up. They've been on hold for nearly half an hour. Maybe one of them's our boy." Jay signaled that the last of the commercials was about to end.

...

"Why *not* Hillary Clinton as president?" Anita in Daly City wanted to know. "I know you would rather shoot yourself in the head than vote for a Democrat, but still! She couldn't be any worse than her husband was. Imagine it: a president is a flagrant womanzier while in office. He gets impeached. And a few years later his wife runs for that same office! Is this a great country or what?"

"Tell you what I like about her," Desirée said. "She's a woman and an elected official. What if the Senate were filled with women? A lot more would get done because women naturally try, when in a position of power, to use their power to improve things for everyone. Men, on the other hand, look at power in terms of money and control."

"So if women took over Congress," asked Anita, "what differences would we see?"

"We would see a huge change in the way American children are treated," said Desirée. "More and better everything: early childhood education, medical care, nutrition. A Senate full of women would consider healthy, optimistic children to be the nation's top priority. They would have better answers to the questions of preventing street crime, unwanted pregnancies and high unemployment."

"I know lots of women, mainly Republicans, who

would disagree with what you just said," Anita told her.

"Maybe. But I know of lots of male politicians who, in order to get elected, spouted the same propaganda we've been hearing for so many years. 'If you'll elect me, I'll resolve all of our major issues.' Have they? Hell, no! They've just talked the talk without being able to walk the walk." She paused. "Remember all the trouble Joycelyn Elders got into when she was surgeon general under Bill Clinton? He had to fire her—actually, it was probably her boss, Donna Shalala, who canned her—because Elders offended so many uptight, upright people. She talked about masturbation and contraception at the United Nations. We have this puritannical, Victorian society in which you just can't talk about sex. That's a taboo subject. We have the highest teen-pregnancy rate in the industrialized world and who knows how many cases of sexually transmitted disease? We tell ourselves that our teenagers don't have sex even though they admit that they do.

"You know the big lie about women's sexuality? It's that we're not supposed to enjoy sex, that we're here to serve men. When they have us barefoot and pregnant in the kitchen, they're in charge. They have all the power. And do you know what men need to know about women's sexuality? That we're sexual beings, yes, but we're *human* beings, not sex objects."

A few more calls followed, all of them brief and not nearly as provocative. Then a voice hissed, "*Desirée.*"

Christina looked at Desirée and nodded. Desirée flashed a sign to Jay, who went back to the commercials. "What do you want?" she asked.

"You know what I want. You killed my best friend."

Desirée swallowed hard. "You must have loved him."

"More than you could ever know. You destroyed him, like you've probably destroyed so many others. So you must die."

He went on in some detail as to what she might expect in the way of retribution when their inevitable meeting occurred but she had stopped listening; she could hear only a voice speaking incomprehensibly.

Christina nodded as soon as Desirée hung up. "It worked. We got a trace."

Desirée blew out a huge breath. "Will this be the beginning of the end of this nightmare?"

"Let's hope so."

. . .

Desirée stared straight ahead as Christina drove her home. The Ragin' Cajun wanted to believe that this had opened the case and now it was almost a matter of time before they caught the caller. But Christina drove on silently, making Desirée feel that there was much the cop wasn't willing to tell her.

By and by they reached Desirée's home. Immediately she saw Harris's car there. Harris, in fact, stood on her front step, smoking a cigarette. Desirée wasn't altogether surprised to see fog blowing across her field of vision and, when she emerged from the car, feel an almost painful chill in the air. Spring in San Francisco.

"Let's go upstairs," said Harris as she approached him.

"Tell me what's happening," she said, making no motion to climb the stairs.

"We didn't get him," he said with the smallest of shrugs. "He called from a pay phone in Fisherman's Wharf."

She sighed. "Back to square one, then."

"No. We're getting closer. He's getting reckless."

"I just want to go inside and crawl into bed," she said. "Let's see if I can dream this away." She darted up the steps as if being pursued by the mystery caller and within a moment was gone.

"Son of a bitch," Harris muttered, unsure if he referred to the caller or the fact that he would not be sleeping anywhere in Desirée's house that night. "I thought we had him. I can't believe he used a pay phone. How did he get through on a goddamn pay phone?"

Christina shrugged. "Maybe next time, as they say. You ready to call it a night?"

"No. I'm gonna stick around here."

"You're off duty right now. Not getting paid. We could call for a uniform to stake out the house."

"No, I'll do this on my own time."

She frowned. "You don't sleep well in cars."

"No," he muttered, "but I wouldn't be able to sleep tonight, no matter where I spent the night."

. . .

In the morning, the fog was everywhere, making Desirée's whole world gray as she looked out the window. Occasionally she wondered if she had made a mistake by accepting the KCA job and moving to San Francisco. She also wondered if she had made a mistake by leaving Louisiana so many years earlier.

New Orleans hadn't been perfect, and her other former cities hadn't made her feel entirely welcome, either, despite high ratings and better paychecks, but she hadn't been harassed in those places. Now and again she yearned to just pack her suitcases and flee, with or without her sister.

She bathed and dressed, then sauntered out into her living room and looked out the front window. Outside was Harris's car. Inside, on her sofa, was Harris, lounging like the laziest man on earth.

"Good morning, sunshine," he said.

Desirée frowned. "How did you get in here?"

"I kicked in the door. Or maybe I jimmied it with my credit card." He smirked. "Or maybe your sister let me in. I can't remember which."

"You're wearing yesterday's clothes," she observed. "You didn't go home last night after I left you on my front steps."

Harris smirked. "You're batting a thousand."

"*Why* didn't you go home last night?"

"Because I didn't want the boogeyman to get you."

"I guess I should thank you," she said.

He shook his head. "Not necessary to thank me."

She sat down on the other end of the sofa. "I was sure you were going to catch him when Christina said the trace turned up a phone number. A phone booth at Fisherman's Wharf? He's smarter than we thought. I sometimes try to visualize what this creep looks like. I keep getting this image of Charles Manson. Just imagine Manson standing there at the phone booth at the Wharf, punching my number and doing his freaky thing while the tourists walk on by."

He shook his head. "He's no Charles Manson or Richard Ramirez. He's probably some clean-cut schlub like that B.T.K. guy from a few years back in Kansas. I have a feeling this caller is someone who can move about freely in this town. Anyway, we'll know soon enough. Right?"

She sighed. "I guess."

"Say," he said, "you want to take it easy today with me? It's my day off."

"I don't really have what most people would call a day off. If I'm not at the station doing my show, I'm preparing for the next show."

"Well, it's time you took a day off. No shift at KCA tonight. I know your schedule by now."

"I'm going to be hosting a class reunion downtown," she said.

"I didn't know talk-show hosts moonlighted as emcees at class reunions."

They usually didn't. In Broadcast House were two stations, KCA and KRCK, the latter being the Bay Area's top-rated FM rock-music station. KRCK's highly popular air personalities were available for live events, and whenever all were committed elsewhere the station would call upstairs to ask a KCA host to take the job. Desirée accepted this one.

"Want to come along as sort of my date?" she asked.

"Sort of your date," he mused. "On one condition."

"Yes?"

"Dinner first. On me."

"OK. But we have to get there early so I can make sure everything's hooked up."

"That's not your job. How will you know that plug A goes into hole B?"

She rolled her eyeballs. "I've been in this business for a decade. I know how to do remotes. I can assemble and break down electrical equipment with the best of them." Then, "Maybe we shouldn't call this a 'date.' That word has *implications*." She thought for a moment. "You know, I lay awake in bed last night, obsessing over that guy's voice on the phone, and I thought I wouldn't survive the night till I started concentrating on you and the help you're giving me, and that made my night go so much better."

He grinned. "Glad I'm good for something."

"While you're feeling helpful, you might also take a look at my plumbing in the bathroom. Something's wrong with it."

"I'm a cop, not a plumber. What makes you think I can fix your leaks?"

"Well, you're a man, and men are inherently good at those kinds of things. My toolbox is in the hall closet. The tools have never been used, since I don't know how to use them. When you're done, let me know. I'll be in my den downstairs."

. . .

Desirée felt giddy whenever she looked at the *Western Broadcasting Company* entry on her bank statement and considered the amount her employer had deposited into her checking account. Her co-workers—and everyone else who read *Billboard*—knew the approximate amount of her salary, although many did not particularly want to know. The other women her age at KCA had modest administrative jobs at, envied her. A degree-less female, under thirty, with a high-paying, top-rated nightly radio show in San Francisco. Who but Desirée Dupree could make such a boast? And who could claim to have spent her entire career in major broadcasting markets?

Sitting in her den, which was really just a poorly conceived third bedroom that was always much too cold to be used for sleeping, she stared at her wad of unpaid bills and wondered how envious her colleagues would be if they knew the true facts of her financial life. Her creditors were many and varied. Golden State Mortgage Corporation. Van Ness Avenue Cars and Trucks. The University of California. Visa, MasterCard and American Express. Next month would be just as bad.

She had lived elsewhere—Chicago and Boston—but had been too preoccupied with day-to-day survival to grow resentful about the high cost of living in those places. San Francisco, too, was a scandalously expensive city to reside in. Buying a house, not just a condominium, was an enterprise few San Franciscans could afford to undertake. Desirée had set aside one day at the end of each month to pay all her creditors. She likened the experience to that of a roller-coaster ride: lofty climbs when her salary was added to her checking account by direct deposit, and equally steep falls as she wrote the monthly checks. She kept two cars on the road—she lacked the heart to make Monique take the bus to and from school although most of the other medical students did so without complaint—and paid her sister's tuition. Both women seldom had more than a few dollars in cash and often lived off debit cards. Life in the Bay Area, she had muttered to herself more than once during these bill-paying sessions, was only for those who had a sense of humor.

But San Francisco was her home now and she quickly developed a sense of permanence. She kept reassuring herself that her present issues would soon resolve themselves: the cops would soon catch her tormentor, Monique would graduate and start paying her own way and Desirée would live happily ever after.

She suddenly felt a cold hand on her shoulder. "Desirée—"

"Hah! Oh!" Desirée grabbed her chest. "Don't sneak up on me like that!"

Harris laughed. "Well, when *you* concentrate, you're really oblivious to all else. The plumbing's all done. Want me to paint your house next?"

"No, but you could do my month's shopping." She was grateful for his help. A large plumbing bill—was there such a thing as a small bill?—would have presented her with one more difficult financial problem. "So, my plumbing is good as new, right?"

"Hardly. Your house is old. So is your plumbing. It's sort of turning to shit, pardon the pun. It'll be OK till it breaks down again."

"Well, since you've been a good boy, how about

if I fix you some lunch? You like P.B. and J. with the crusts removed?"

He rubbed his stomach. "Yummy! Then you can read to me from *Harry Potter*."

She ignored this. "By the way, what *was* wrong with my plumbing?"

"You wouldn't understand."

"Then why do *you* understand it?"

"Because I am a man. Besides, I have a rental property to look after and it helps to be something of a handyman." He pulled her up out of her seat and kissed her. "I'm also handy *this* way. I am a man of many talents."

"This is not the talent you're here to show off," she said, prying herself away from him. She looked at him levelly. "I need you to be a cop. Understand? Maybe we can pursue these other avenues later. But now I need you to catch a perp before I lose my mind."

"We'll get him," he said. "It's just a matter of time. You see, these kinds of guys, stalkers, get very sloppy after they've been after the same person for a while. Or maybe they secretly want to get caught because they know they're being bad and they want to stop doing that stuff but don't have the willpower to stop themselves, so they make it easy for us to catch them and make them stop. It's all very sick and twisted, catch these creeps who lurk out there in the night." He ran a hand through his hair. "God, I love being a cop. This job can be too much fun sometimes. I'd probably do it for free, or I'd pay them to let me do it."

# CHAPTER 7

In the Pacific Palace Hotel's Gold Rush Room, nearly every member of the John Monroe High Class of 1980 was present. Mirrored balls suspended from the ceiling cast blobs of light on the walls as dance music pounded and strobe lights flickered on undulating bodies.

The Ragin' Cajun, Mistress of Ceremonies, stood at the front of the room, surrounded by a barrier of electronic equipment. Nearby, watching her, Harris sipped a Diet Coke and politely declined some female guests' persistent invitations to dance.

Desirée looked spectacular in a Michael Jackson-style sequined tuxedo with flood pants and Day-Glo white socks, her hair chopped off above the shoulders, then scissored, teased and gelled into a fashionable mess. A MacIntosh laptop computer sat open glowing before her, packed with countless dance songs. At the other end of the room sat an identical laptop for partiers to electronically send song and dedication requests to Desirée.

The Gold Rush Room was dark, sweaty and exhilarating, filled with handsome dancers. Desirée, looking around, thought it was all just too much fun. Work was not supposed to be fun and fun was not supposed to be work. The room looked just like the Brooklyn discothéque in *Saturday Night Fever,* the favorite title in her DVD collection. Sometimes, when tired of being in public life, she watched John Travolta with his polyester hair and ice cream suit and yearned to play Stephanie to his Tony Manero—she wanted to be twenty, living with her family, hanging out with her girlfriends and dancing till dawn every weekend. Sometimes such a humble existence seemed vastly preferable to being Queen Bitch of talkradio.

These Monroe High alumni hardly seemed disappointed to have a controversial broadcaster as their celebrity emcee. Local media personalities, contractually obligated only to welcome the guests and shake a few hands, as often as not departed minutes into the event. Not Desirée. Certainly they appreciated having her there; the men apparently considered her even sexier than her image on KCA's Website. They bought liquid courage at the cash bar and, wanting to get up close and personal, came up to her swigging from bottles of Beck's and Corona. She flirted back just enough, then drifted over behind the computer.

"Look at these requests," she said, pulling Harris over. "Bee Gees. Peter Frampton. Pat Benatar. Are these people living in a time warp? What's their problem? I would have guessed they'd want songs by Britney Spears, Madonna and Celine Dion."

He shook his head. "Dunno. Idiots. But who cares? Let's dance." He took her by the hand, led her to the dance floor and twirled her in his arms.

"You know how to boogie," she shouted. "But I'm here to work, not dance. If we keep this up, I won't be able to run the music and lights."

"Computer does that for you." But then he

danced her back to her post behind the computer. "Back to work. Want something to drink?"

"Not right now." She fiddled with the computer, her hips swaying to the irresistible dance beat. *Goddamn, I love to party. Especially these parties. Reunions. Wish this was mine. I'd like to see my old friends again, even if we weren't exactly friends back then. I wasn't all that likable when I was that age.*

"These people graduated in Eighty. Reaganomics. The Forty-niners. *Ordinary People* cleaned up at the Oscars."

"You sound like the World Almanac," said Harris.

"It's my job." Then she looked down at the computer screen again and punched Harris in the shoulder. She gestured for him to look at the screen.

*I enjoyed seeing you tonight. The next time I see you it will be the last time.*

*He's here,* she mouthed to Harris, her face now frozen with fear.

He pulled her to the nearest exit; presently they were in a quiet corner of the building. "You want to call it a night? We can get someone else to cover for you."

She shook her head. "No, I'll just tough it out."

"Let me make a few phone calls. Cop stuff. In the lobby. Let's go."

He escorted her out. On their way to the door they were stopped by a handsome, sweating Chinese man in a suit, obviously one of the graduates of 1980. He grabbed her hands and pumped them in a most enthusiastic handshake. "Desirée Dupree! Desirée Dupree!" he gushed. "Ragin' Cajun, givin' 'em shit! Wow!" He took a breath. "I'm Wes Lee—no relation to Bruce. I'm head of the reunion committee—the guy who organized this craziness. Last year I lost two hundred pounds—I got divorced! Get it?"

He gave her arm a playful slap. "Anyway," he continued, "I sell yachts. I read *Billboard*, so I know you make megabucks. Young lady with megabucks should have a yacht for weekend fun, right? Here's my card. You want a good deal on a yacht, you just come see Wes Lee. Hear?" He gave her his biggest, toothiest smile and darted away.

"I hear," she murmured to the ghost of Wes Lee.

"Who the hell was that?" Harris asked.

"Oh, just some guy trying to sell me a yacht," she said.

"I get that all the time. Isn't it annoying?" He steered her into the hotel's vast, opulent lobby and she sat while he made a call on his Blackberry. She was still trying to believe the caller had gotten into the Gold Rush Room.

I must not think about this right now, she cautioned herself. I must think about something else. She thought about the gleaming salmon-and-turquoise lobby she was in. She had read *City for Sale* and brought up the issue of gentrification many times on the air. The Pacific Palace, south of Market

Street, was one of the indirect results of a massive redevelopment plan started by Fairmont Hotel owner Ben Swig in the 1950s. The project accelerated in the 1970s because of San Francisco Redevelopment Agency head Justin Herman. Yerba Buena Center, Moscone Center, PacBell Park, the Pacific Palace...all more or less were the offspring of Swig and Herman.

TransWorld Hotels boasted that its Pacific Palace was grandest hotel west of Las Vegas. Desirée thought San Francisco needed the Pacific Palace as much as it needed another major earthquake. Its marbled lobby seemed big enough for a U2 concert; its more expensive suites were said to be affordable only to the richest celebrities and Asian businessmen.

San Francisco was hotel crazy. As Bay Area radio's Current Big Thing, Desirée had already attended broadcasting functions at the city's other famous hotels—the Fairmont, Mark Hopkins, Huntington, Clift—and when the Fairmont closed for a time because of a strike, some KCA hosts exploited the issue by devoting entire hours to San Francisco tourism and labor disputes. Desirée, indifferent to the Fairmont, did *her* shows about mentally ill, drug-addicted Vietnam veterans who spent their nights shivering in sleeping bags in the Civic Center. She fumed about the HIV-positive boy hustlers who lurked in Polk Street doorways, slept in Market Street grindhouse movie theaters and urinated in the gutters. She concluded that the city's colossal, longstanding woes were things everyone, from the most astute social worker to the most casual person on the street, already knew about but felt powerless to alleviate. Still, the topic made for compelling radio and the Ragin' Cajun's ratings stayed high.

Harris slipped his Blackberry back into his pocket. "I just called in this incident. Nothing we can do about that message in the laptop. We can't stop the party and haul everyone down to the station for questioning, even if he's still there."

She watched as other couples entered and exited the Gold Rush Room. The young lions and their women. Could one of them be the caller? She still thought of him as a Charles Manson type and nearly giggled as she pictured him traipsing in—smelly, long-haired and wild-eyed, escorted by a few of his spaced-out, bald teenaged girlfriends with crosses carved between their glazed, vacant eyes.

No, he wasn't another Manson. He could be anyone, anywhere, moving about freely. He knew where she lived; he'd been by her house, had her phone number. Would she wake up in the middle of the night to find him standing over her, wanting to be the last thing she saw before she died?

"So what are our options?" she asked.

He shrugged. "Call it a night."

"He crashed this reunion and threatened me through the computer. What's it mean?"

"It means," Harris said, keeping his voice low, "he's a brazen son of a bitch who's daring us to catch him. And he's making it increasingly easy for us to do that."

"But *when*?"

"Maybe the next time he contacts you. He doesn't realize how close we are. Or maybe he does and he secretly wants us to bust him. It's hard to tell what goes through their minds." He shrugged. "But, of course, before he messes with *you* he's gonna have to get past *me*. Don't know how he'll do *that*."

"You cops," she said, "act like such badasses."

"We *are* such badasses." He gestured to the Gold Rush Room. "Let's go back inside. Maybe you've got something really funky to play in that computer. We can do some freaking."

Desirée threw back her head and laughed. "Dream *on,* Dirty Harry."

. . .

They didn't call it a night. They went back inside and Desirée finished her evening's work. The scary message on the computer seemed, if anything, to empower her. She perused the dedications and scanned the crowd, looking alert and rhythmic, her hips swaying to the music.

Harris mused as he watched her from a dozen steps away. What kind of wife would she make? What sort of mother? He wanted a woman with blazing intelligence, good humor and quirky observations, and to have a son, not a daughter, who was good and obedient, full of skill and virtue.

But then he reminded himself of the impertinence of such matters. He wasn't there to assess her marital fitness. He could wait till later—once they became engaged. If Desirée didn't know that Harris was her future husband, that was *her* hard luck. She likely would catch on soon enough.

First job, though, was catching the caller. The guy *wanted* to be caught, Harris figured. Caught and punished. Knowing where Desirée lived and worked had given the guy ample opportunity to kill her by now. Men at this reunion freely came by to chat up Desirée; anybody could have walked right up and blown her away before Harris could react. What then? Would the killer have the good sense to shoot himself before Harris arrested him? For this caller, the alternative to dying on the floor of the Gold

Rush Room next to Desirée Dupree, of course, was a life sentence at San Quentin or, worse, Folsom. Harris knew about those places because he had helped send enough guys there.

He thought for a moment about the murder of John Lennon outside the Dakota apartment building. Mark David Chapman, the 26-year-old gunman, had allowed himself to be arrested and incarcerated for life at Rikers Island rather than simply killing himself on that evening in December of 1980. Even the guys committing lesser crimes, such as robbers of jewelry stores, who at gunpoint obtained Rolexes and cash, were usually apprehended before they could leave the store. If you were going to commit a felony and lacked competency or luck—or both, as most would-be robbers did—you probably would get caught. And if you started shooting, Harris believed, you needed to save one bullet for yourself. If they took you alive, you went to prison, to face years of psychiatric disorders resulting from nighttime shivs and gang rapes. He shook his head and sighed. Crime, he thought, sure doesn't pay.

Just then he saw Christina enter the reunion. Princess Diana couldn't have turned more heads. She was wearing the simplest black dress, but there was nothing simple about the way she filled it out, breasts bouncing and hips swaying.

"Christina," said Harris, "you are just too damn sexy."

She made a face. "Tell me about it. I had a date tonight with this guy and you do *not* want to hear about it."

"Like I said, you're too damn sexy."

She looked around. "So, how's tonight going?"

"Not boring, I would say."

"Your assignment is...what a tuxedo."

"That's the future Mrs. Cavanaugh you're talking about," Harris said in a voice that made it clear that he wasn't altogether kidding.

"Does she know she's spoken for?"

"She'll figure it out eventually."

Christina eyed him. "Kidding aside, we have a perp to catch. Remember that."

"I remember. If I forget, I'll just remind myself that he's here tonight and left a nasty message on her computer." Harris realized just how loud he needed to be in order to be heard over the music, so he stopped talking.

The reunion was in its final minutes. Desirée, determined to get everyone on the dance floor for the last few songs, chose the three tracks with the most irresistible beats. By the last one, all the partiers were jacketless; ties were undone, faces shiny with sweat and only the radio princess and two hardboiled cops were standing still.

"Class of Eighty, you guys rock!" Desirée howled into the microphone. "In another five years, we'll do it again. OK?" There was a huge roar of agreement.

"I think they liked you," Harris said.

"I think they liked each other," Desirée said, already unhooking the equipment and turning off the computer even though doing so wasn't her job. "Hope they make some effort at staying in touch. That's the point of these reunions."

She stared at the equipment, which she had readied for its return trip to Broadcast House. "Damn, that was fun even though I didn't actually know anyone here." She laughed. "Maybe it was fun *because* I didn't know anyone here. If I had gone to school with them, I probably would have been so busy bragging that I wouldn't have been in the mood to dance and enjoy myself."

"It was fun because it was fun," said a voice behind Desirée.

"Kelvin!" she said, turning around. "Don't you ever go home?"

"No, going home is against the terms of my contract. I can guess the sort of crap you were playing tonight. It makes me glad that I'm the boss of a talk station, not a rock station."

"Hey, the class of Eighty loved that crap tonight.

So, any particular reason you're here?"

"No." He looked around and said, "You know, I met my wife in high school. These reunions are a guilty pleasure of mine."

Desirée smirked. "Especially since everyone at your reunions probably knows you're King Shit at KCA."

Kelvin laughed. "Well, there's that, too. And as King Shit, I'm here to inform you that, effective immediately, you have a severe case of laryngitis and are unfit to work." He smiled without mirth.

"I'm fine," Desirée said. "Really."

"You'd better go see a doctor about that laryngitis before it gets any worse. If I see you around the station tomorrow or the day after, consider yourself canned."

"Christ," she muttered.

"Yes, that's me, I was born in a manger to a virgin. Your time off is necessary. We get this harassing-caller matter cleared up and you'll be back on the air. Until then..." He threw up his hands.

"Time to go," Harris said, taking her by the hand. "I'm sure the flunkies can take the equipment back to the station."

In the hotel's parkade, she said, "Now what? Seems my boss has just laid me off for a few days."

"Me too. We can put our heads together and contemplate our respective futures." They reached his car. "In you go."

She slid onto the passenger's seat and he started up the engine. Music blared from the stereo, melancholy and ancient. "What the hell is *that?*" she asked.

"Guess."

She listened for a moment, then nodded. "Miles Davis. *Sketches of Spain.*"

Harris grinned. "Right. A jazz classic. I need this after all the shit you played for those clowns tonight."

"I don't like jazz. I like that dance shit I played all night."

"Well, you should learn to appreciate fine music. It's good for the soul."

"So is going to the Sunday service at St. Mary's, but I'm nowhere in sight when the church bells ring." She paused. "Did you set this up? With Kelvin coming by and telling me to take time off?"

"Would you be angry if I did?"

"Maybe."

"Then no, I didn't. But you do need a breather."

"Thank you, Dr. Cavanaugh."

"Just trying to make myself useful. After all, my job is to serve and protect."

"You seem to think your real job is to seduce harassed radio hosts." But she would welcome the time off. At home were new issues of magazines on her coffee table—*Billboard, Variety* and *Architectural Digest* plus an untouched copy of *San Francisco Today*. She liked to read up on the city she lived in but so rarely visited in any meaningful way.

*What did I miss seeing in Boston?* she asked herself as Harris drove them out of the hotel's parkade. *Damn near everything. Sis went to school and I went to work. Did I walk through the Commons? Maybe once. See the Sox or Celtics play? Nope. Didn't make any friends, either, and damned if I could tell a San Franciscan five things to see and do in Beantown, or tell a tourist five things to do here in Baghdad by the Bay. Back in Boston, I just read The Globe, listened to the other hosts and licked my finger to see which way the wind was blowing. No, that's not true; I didn't test the wind. I didn't care what the radio listeners of Boston thought. I* gave them my libertarian politics and Buddhist worldview because that's what I really *believed in. I was no kiss-ass; I cared about what Desirée Dupree thought, and that's what's saved me because it made me different from the others.*

*The demographics in San Francisco say my audience is affluent, with the typical priorities: power, profits, prestige, pleasure, private property. If they don't like what I'm about, fuck 'em.* She smiled at how seriously she could take herself. *Kelvin can fire me and I'll just have to find a new career. Maybe even expand my social circle. Have more fun, chill out.*

She closed her eyes and took a deep breath. Harris's car smelled fresh and new, of plastic and rubber and authentic leather. The jazz music sounded less abrasive now. Desirée's tuxedo, in which she was still dressed, felt damp and sticky; she could smell her own stink. Her bra strap was digging into her underarm and her leg muscles and buttocks were sore, tired from prolonged anxiety and the dancing she'd done. She seldom worked out, finding repetitive, intense exercise deeply unpleasant and considering it unnecessary at her age. She also felt drowsy now, her eyelids getting impossibly heavy, and she closed her eyes for the briefest moment.

When she opened them again, they were speeding along now. They were nowhere near KCA or her house. The sky was the deepest black and nothing was familiar. Looming above the roadway was a huge

206

Toyota billboard lit up with the admonition PLEASE KEEP YOUR EYES ON THE ROAD. She took her eyes off the road to look over at Harris, who returned her glance.

"Sleeping beauty," he said. "Did you know you snore?"

"Where are we going?" Desirée snapped. "We're nowhere near KCA or my home. We're not even in San Francisco anymore!"

"We're on Highway One southbound."

"The Pacific Coast Highway?"

"Yes, ma'am."

"I thought you were driving me home. So why are we going down the coast? Where exactly are we going?"

"To my shack."

"What? I thought you lived in San Francisco. You showed it to me. Remember?"

"Well, can't a fella have *two* places?"

"A 'shack'? I didn't think you could have a shack in a fancy place like Carmel."

"I got a special permit to build one. As long as the wind doesn't blow too hard, my shack should stay in one place. If my fancy-ass neighbors don't like it, that's *their* problem."

She shook her head. "No, I refuse to do this. Monique will wonder where I've gone."

"Monique will be glad to have the weekend away from you. She told me so when she packed your overnight bag, which is in my trunk. She wants you to say hi to the other Dirty Harry down here. He used to be the town's mayor, you know."

Desirée snarled. "This was all a conspiracy. That's why Kelvin came by the reunion to tell me to take time off."

"Yeah, something like that. I think you'll like Carmel. Been there yet?"

"No, too busy with other things."

"You'll like it."

"Turn back immediately," she demanded. "I am not going with you. I want to spend this weekend in my own bed."

"Maybe next weekend we can do that."

"Don't be funny, Cavanaugh. This must be illegal. Kidnapping or something."

"You're right. I'll arrest myself when we get back to San Francisco after the weekend."

She crossed her arms and thrust out her chin. "I'm not going into your shack. I'm not going to leave this car."

He laughed. "Gonna sleep in the car? You'll catch cold. And what if you gotta go to the bathroom? It will be an awfully long weekend for you."

"Well, I'll tell you this right now: I am going to have just a really shitty time."

"Interesting choice of words, considering you won't be going to the bathroom for the entire weekend."

# CHAPTER 8

Desirée still didn't think it was funny. Maybe he thought he was doing her a favor by holding her hostage for the weekend in his "shack" by the sea. He had abducted her; that was the simple truth of it. As far as she knew, abduction in modern-day California was a felony, even for good-looking cops from rich families, and she would make damn sure the bastard got *his* when the time came.

But for now she was going to be the most frigid human being he had ever met. She would curl up in the car if she had to and not speak one word to him throughout the weekend. She would make him regret his actions for the rest of his life. And she would get some satisfaction in doing so.

That was how she felt until they reached Carmel. She had thought of the town as being covered in fog much of the time, but when they arrived the sky was full of huge stars blazing under a full moon.

In addition to being a kidnaper, he was a liar. The shack wasn't what he had told her; it was more like a cabin, a big one. To her, a shack was a tarpaper booth where you slept on the floor. Harris's place was made of wood that looked as solid as steel but warm as fur. It was two stories tall and appeared to offer a breathtaking view of the Pacific Ocean. She wondered how it might feel to retire here, to stop being the Ragin' Cajun and worrying about weirdo phone callers. Just spend her many remaining days and nights in this marvelous wooden home. Why hadn't Harris stopped busting heavies and done exactly that?

But she said nothing. She just emerged from the car and took a deep breath through her nose. What was that odd smell? She sniffed again. Fresh air.

"Quaint," she said, marching towards the front door. Harris could get her overnight bag, if he knew what was good for him. The guy was full of surprises. Money, looks and smarts. His family was one of San Francisco's oldest and most prominent. He had this little piece of paradise just a few hours away, where he could sit back and read big philosophy books all day. But he kept on working. Go figure people. She would never be able to understand them and their motivations.

She ambled out onto the porch and was instantly bitten by a tiny gust of chilly wind. Good. She didn't want to be comfortable. She wanted things to complain about; she wanted him to see her disgust.

"Here's your bag," he said. "Let's go inside."

She tried to think of something snide to say as he opened the front door.

She wanted to tell him how much nerve he had in taking her down there and what a dreadful time she would have.

She would really tell him off.

He turned on the light.

"Wow," she said.

The main room at the cabin's center was huge, an open-gabled structure with rough-hewn beams and a charming granite fireplace. Thick, cushy furniture was arranged around it. Its freestanding chimney rose up through the high, lofted ceiling. Above, a balcony swept the width of the room, keeping with the theme of open space and wood. In contrast, the walls were a simple white, accented with glossy built-in shelves and many-paned doors and windows.

This, naturally, was nothing like his home in San Francisco. The cabin was about enjoying the open space, while his Nob Hill place was about making the most of a fairly small apartment. The cabin's wide planked floors were bare. A set of gleaming steps marched straight to the next level. Beside the fireplace was an open woodbox stacked with split logs. A touch of whimsy was added by grinning brass dragons that served as andirons.

"Don't worry about the cold," Harris said. "In a minute or two it'll be so warm in here that you'll want to walk around in your birthday suit." She wouldn't stop giving him the cold shoulder once hers warmed up. She would also get hungry soon, and was he prepared for that? "If you get hungry, the kitchen is about ten feet away. It's always stocked with stuff. Help yourself. I'm sure you'll find something you like."

She had eaten lightly at the reunion and her stomach was beginning to growl. But she said nothing; she simply watched as Harris stocked the fireplace and started a fire as effortlessly as if he had been doing so all his life. He was turning out to be quite a handyman, she thought, even though he could easily pay someone else to do those things for him.

He looked her way, as if acknowledging that they were not yet on speaking terms. Well, they would be, soon enough, because their setting was too charming for her to maintain her anger.

"Upstairs are two guest bedrooms. Choose whichever one you like. There's a sleeping porch outside but you may wake up in the middle of the night with a deer cuddling you."

Now you're mocking me, she thought. Well, up yours, too, pal. She took her overnight bag and marched upstairs.

Each of the bedrooms was immaculate and finely appointed. She chose the most feminine-looking room and went inside, locking the door behind her. She had seen *Architectural Digest* pictorials of inns that weren't nearly as attractive. She set her bag on the bed and looked inside, to see what Monique had considered appropriate for Desirée's weekend at Harris's place.

She smiled at the heavily napped purple LSU sweatshirt that had become one of her most prized possessions. The cowboy boots were nice, too. The perfume and rouge would come in handy although she seriously doubted that Harris would be worth the trouble. Instead of her usual Giants or 49ers jersey, she found a Frederick's of Hollywood black silk-and-lace teddy that couldn't have blocked a sneeze.

*Don't do anything I wouldn't do. But if you do, wear this. Love, M.*

Good old Monique, always allying herself with the enemy, or at least trying to get her older sister laid. Well, this item was not the sort of thing Desirée had any intention of wearing and she wasn't about to start wearing it here with Dirty Harry snoozing away just down the hall. Still, it was lovely bit of silk, what there was of it. Desirée normally didn't have such things. Her closet was full of Gap slacks, skirts and blouses that were comfortable and moderately dressy, things in which she felt most and she had bought a couple of impractical but stylish Wilkes Bashford outfits to wear to business appearances as KCA's star-of-the-moment. So she promised herself she would slip on the teddy because her sister had bought it for her and therefore it was a gift and Desirée knew it was rude not to accept gifts.

She could feel the room fill with heat and gratefully shed her clothes to climb into that big tub in the bathroom. Pour in some bubble bath and soak away the night's difficulties, then climb into that big bed to sleep away whatever remained of her troubles.

That was the plan. She would be selfish and cold towards Harris to teach him a lesson. But then she nearly fell asleep as the perfumed water caressed her all over. Pleasing images of herself floated across her consciousness: at the reunion, stylsih and agile, being admired by all; standing in her favorite corner of the broadcast booth, staring out at the calm dark water as fog drifted across the Bay Bridge; the sight of Monique bounding into their living room after getting an A on a midterm examination.

Her eyelids got so heavy that she feared falling asleep in the tub. Getting out, she toweled herself dry and put on the teddy. It fit just right, in all the right places. She looked in the mirror, thinking, *Didn't know I could be such a sexy thing.* She also wondered how Harris might react to seeing her this way. How he would peel the teddy from her and feel and smell the delicious moistness of her skin. A little softcore porn movie started up on the screen behind her eyes: *Dirty Harry Meets the Ragin' Cajun.* She cringed and shook away the image.

*No can do, girlfriend,* she told herself, changing back into her robe and leaving the bathroom. *You're not here to fantasize about seductions and cops; you're here to collect yourself until they catch the bad guy. Bedtime for Desirée. Erase all your thoughts, get the ether to dissipate from your agitated mind.*

At the nightstand she found a Baccarat brandy snifted filled with a chocolate-colored liquid. Tia Maria. She sipped it. Yummy. She saw herself in the mirror—soft and dark, supple, ready for loving. Was all this part of Harris's plan for this weekend? If so, he had predicted her behavior accurately. She put the teddy back on and left the bedroom in search of him.

He sat downstairs in front of the fireplace with a tattered copy of Kant's *A Critique of Pure Reason,* a book he had battled for years, understanding it one day but mystified by it the next. Tonight was one of the difficult times. He also wondered what Desirée was doing upstairs. Was she thinking of him? Did she enjoy the Tia Maria he had set down on her nightstand?

The interest was mutual, he assured himself. He knew when a woman was attracted to him and when she wasn't—and usually she *was*—and he was quite sure Desirée was even if she pretended she wasn't. His attraction to her wasn't entirely sexual, either, although much of it was. He looked at the dust jacket of his book and said silently to the portrait of Immanuel Kant, *I'm in love with her and she'll love me, too. You'll see. And if she didn't see, I'll point it out to her. She will love me. I am a lovable man. Right, Manny?*

He then listened intently to the trumpet playing of Miles Davis. He had listened to *Sketches of Spain* for years and knew a work of music was a masterpiece when he could listen to it a hundred times or more and hear it differently each time. Then he gazed at the fire for a few minutes and felt the deepest bliss. Miles Davis over a fire down in Carmel was one of his greatest pleasures. It was so special because in a few days he would be back busting heavies in San Francisco, where he had seen the worst of human behavior—raiding glory holes and gay bathhouses, processing the crime scene in which a man has gone berserk with his handgun in a five-person murder-suicide. Harris Cavanaugh was a man who craved his adrenalin fixes as much as Tenderloin addicts loved speedballs. But after a week or two of patrolling the mean streets of San Francisco, he needed to escape for a couple of days with a crackling fire and Miles Davis. But after those two days, he needed to get back to those mean streets for that chemical rush.

He also found that he needed a fix named Desirée Dupree, and it seemed only natural and inevitable to have her down there in his weekend refuge. The attraction was mutual, he assured himself. She simply wasn't ready to admit it. For whatever screwed-up reason, she refused to participate in life. She ran away by burying herself in her work, worrying about the damned competition—the Arbitron ratings indicated she had nothing to fret about—and playing mother hen to her sister. Monique was nobody's baby. Couldn't the freakin' Ragin' Cajun see that Monique needed only to do her own thing without having to answer to Big Sis—

He looked up, open-mouthed, and saw her standing there.

"What's goin' on?" she asked, as if trying to sound like Marvin Gaye. The ludicrousness of what she was doing had very nearly compelled her to call off this little confrontation, but there she stood, facing him as he sat near the fireplace.

"Just chillin'," he said, answering her clichéd question with one of his own. He felt the heat from the fireplace settle into his groin. "Or warmin.'"

"I want to talk to you," she said. "I know why you brought me here. It's for my own benefit. I suppose I should be grateful, and I am. But to abduct me like you did? You're taking the law into your own hands. I'm going to do my next show about you: Dirty Harry the Vigilante."

"I'll be sure to listen in."

She arched an eyebrow. "So...?"

He couldn't take his eyes off her teddy and what

little it covered.

"Jesus, you bring me down here against my will and then don't have the courtesy to pay attention to me while I bitch about it."

"So just keep bitching."

"The air must be thin down here. You seem to have trouble maintaining the simplest conversation."

Harris picked up his copy of *A Critique of Pure Reason* and began smacking himself with it.

"What the hell are you doing?"

"I'm whacking myself in the head."

"Why?"

"Because it feels so good when I stop," he said.

"You're very weird," she said. Then she stared past him, apparently just lost in her own thoughts. He stared again at her, noting the slim lines of her body in that teddy. Her breasts were bigger than he had thought—bigger and more supple. Her hips also had an appealing breadth he had not noticed before.

Before he realized what he was doing, he got up and stood before her, placing his hands on her shoulders.

"What are you looking at?" she snapped.

"I'm looking at you. Maybe you shouldn't wear things like that."

"It's just a teddy."

"Then maybe you shouldn't wear that body."

"Monique put it in my overnight bag. I wouldn't have bought such a thing for myself."

"So I've noticed. It's not your style. Your style, frankly, turns me off. But this thing you're wearing is—"

"The reason I came downstairs," she said, "is to get on the same page, so to speak, about why we are here. We need to agree on some ground rules."

"And you want to have a mature, matter-of-fact dialogue with me while you stand there wearing this little piece of nothing, looking like an O'Farrell Theatre stripper."

"Maybe that's why you're not thinking so clearly right now. All your blood has gone down to the little head."

"Mission accomplished. If you want to take it farther with me, yes, we can do that. But afterwards you'll have to acknowledge that it was your decision. Or did you come out here dressed like this, hoping I would just sweep you off to bed and that you could tell yourself I took advantage of you?"

"These are not small decisions to make," she said.

"You mean about sex? Yes, they are small decisions. People make these decisions every night. All you have to do is say yes."

"Would you mind taking your hands off my shoulders?"

He let his hands remain there for a moment longer, then let them fall away, as if to say, *Have it your way*. He looked at her and she returned his gaze, then stepped towards him and snaked her arms about his shoulders. "I've made my decision. Guess what it is."

He took her mouth as if claiming a prize. Her body, in his arms, felt supple as a cat's. He felt breathless, as if punched in the solar plexus, as he moved his hands around the silkiness of her back. He wanted her, wanted all of her, wanted her right now and forever. As he tugged at her shoulder strap, she took his hand and led him upstairs to her bedroom.

She didn't want to lose this momentum. She didn't want him to have misgivings about any of this. This had to be the most exciting time of his life. The best, most memorable time.

His skin was softer and warmer than she would have thought, almost in some ways like a baby's. She wanted to take it slow and easy with him, but if he wanted it otherwise, she would do it his way.

She heard a guttural moan rush up from the depths of him as she tore off his clothes. He said *Now* and she understood, the two of them entwined and writhing in an instant.

His face contorted in ecstasy and agony and he repeatedly thrust. To make their loving last longer he tried to restrain himself until she wrapped her legs around him, holding him prisoner, forcing him to explode.

She lay after their loving, spent and delighted, sensing his breath.

"What was that all about?"

"I thought you wanted it fast."

"I did. But not that fast," he said.

"Well, I just thought..." She sighed. "I guess I'm out of practice."

"You need to try harder," he told her. When she got out of bed, he said, "Are you going somewhere?"

"To sleep." She put the teddy back on and added, "Maybe this wasn't such a good idea. Just another mistake."

Harris responded by getting up and locking the door.

"I don't want to spend the rest of the night in here with you," she said.

"That's a damn shame," he said.

She stared up at him, thinking, I've made him mad. He's not kidding around, either. It takes sex to make someone this mad. "Was my performance unsatisfactory? I never pretended I was a porn star."

"I didn't say I wanted one. Anyway, in case you haven't noticed, sex is sort of a two-person activity. You aren't there to perform; you're there to have a special experience with someone."

"Well," she said, "maybe if we each find someone special to have that special experience with, it will be that special experience we're suppose to have. Now, let me just go back to my room and go to sleep. Tomorrow's another day."

He said nothing. He stepped over and turned out the lights.

"What's the idea?" she asked.

"We're making our own little porn movie. The camera's hidden. This is take two. We'll do it by moonlight."

"Apparently you weren't listening. I said I wanted to go to sleep."

"Oh, I *was* listening. I just altered your plans somewhat." Sensing her resentment, he added, "I'm just trying to make you feel more comfortable. Bedroom humor, you know." Then, "You are where you're supposed to be, Desirée. Down here, with me. Away from the craziness in the city that brought us together."

*I won't be sweet-talked*, she wanted to say.

"I'm going to show you what love is," he said, slipping the shoulder strap from her teddy. "You need to know what I am here to teach."

"You're going to teach me love?" she asked.

"If you're willing to learn. I'll teach you to be yourself, to love yourself and let others love you."

She tried to resist him. "We already did this."

He held her more tightly. "That was sex. Now it's time for love." He kissed her again, harder. Her heart thundered. "Not this..."

"Then what?" he murmured.

But she had no answer. She had no thoughts or emotions. She had no sense at all of being alive.

"I can offer you some options," he said. "I can do what I know, and I know a lot. You can close your eyes and open your mind. You can experience this with me, then make up your mind which parts you'd like to experience again."

He did not give her time to answer. He plunged his mouth down onto hers, inundating her with kisses. "Wild love," he murmured in her ear. "Desperate, obsessive, willfully blind. Love, as love at its truest is. No future, no past. Only here and now."

He kissed the tops of her breasts, marveling at the silken skin he found there. Her heart pounded, her pulse raced, but she remained motionless.

With excruciating patience, he undid the teddy. She arched her back and threw back her head to scream but merely shuddered. He wanted to be fast and greedy but forced himself to be slow, pulling back the hint of silk and kissing the edges of her generous breasts.

"What's the matter?"

Desirée swallowed hard. "I didn't know it could be this way."

"You mean this good?"

She shrugged.

"You've been doing it the wrong way. Or doing it with the wrong people."

"You're mocking me."

"No mockery. Just soliciting praise. Wanted you to acknowledge that my technique is superior to yours. If you don't want to admit it now, we've got the whole weekend." He smirked. "I'm gonna make you my love slave."

# CHAPTER 9

Desirée felt drowsy as she sighed and looked out the window at the Pacific Ocean. Harris was right; the view was spectacular. He had, right down here, a home and a lifestyle that movies were made about. This was the California Good Life, and the guy who lived that life was still young enough to enjoy it to the fullest, except that he had decided to limit his time here to the weekends and spent the rest of his time in San Francisco as a cop. Desirée couldn't imagine why Harris had chosen to keep his time in paradise limited to weekends. Go figure people.

The window was large. She could see the unreal expanse of the Pacific, stretching on forever, looking calm and warm and inviting but probably deceptively cold and filled with sharks one might encounter if one went in for a swim, as Desirée was not about to do. Around these parts deer roamed and tourists gawked. The California sun, Harris told her, was mysteriously absent most of the time. Well, you couldn't have everything.

"You have a nice little shack here, Dirty Harry."

"I had a feeling you'd like it." He had a feeling, also, that she would come down with him often enough to consider this house her second home.

"Did you have it built or build it yourself? Or just pop out your checkbook and buy it?"

"I had the logs shipped in from Montana. God, was that ever expensive." He laughed, as at the memory of some costly, pointless teenaged adventure. "Then I pretty much hammered it all together myself."

"You should come down here a lot more often. It's wonderful down here."

"Oh, I come down here more often than you think. Especially when I start letting the world drive me nuts. This place, as you can see, bears no relation to the real world." Then, "My folks also like to use this place now and again."

"Do your parents live in San Francisco?"

"No, Palo Alto. Stanford country. Well, actually they're homeless. They travel, travel and travel..."

She eyed him. "You seem like a smart enough guy. Why aren't you running the family empire?"

"I'm plenty smart—in my own way. Want to know about law enforcement? I'm your man. I also know my way around philosophy and a few other subjects. But if you want to make money, find someone else." He chuckled. "If you want to turn a large fortune into a small one, put Harris Cavanaugh in charge."

"So," she asked, "who's in charge of managing all that Cavanaugh money?"

"My sister Bonnie and a few cousins. Tough, cold, intelligent bastards with M.B.A. degrees."

She smirked. "And how do these tough, cold, intelligent bastards feel about your line of work?"

"Hey, they know I'm happy, and they know that happiness isn't the easiest thing to find in this world." He hugged himself. "Damn, it's getting really cold out here. Let's go back inside."

Presently they were in the kitchen. Desirée sniffed loudly and said, "What's that nice smell?"

"I've got some stew cooking," Harris said. He walked over to the stove and lifted the lid of a chrome pot. "Coming along real nice. Be ready soon."

"It's a little late to ask, but would you like some help with it?"

"Nope, it's a done deal. You can cook tomorrow."

"I make a bitchin' sandwich, remember?" she said. "Or were you lying when you said you didn't like it?"

"I guess peanut butter and jelly is an acquired taste."

She guessed that she had made him his first-ever peanut butter and jelly sandwich. His people didn't eat that stuff. They didn't cook much, either. There was hired help for that. She also guessed that Harris's mother hadn't changed too many diapers over the years, either. There were people you could hire to do most of life's dirty deeds.

"Take off your scarf and stay a while," he said.

"OK." She did as told and said, "Now what?"

"Drink." He handed her a glass of red wine. "You seem to be letting anxiety get the better of you again despite being here with me. Or maybe because of being here with me. Let's go sit down by the fire and check this out."

You don't miss much, do you? Desirée wanted to say. No wonder you're such a good inspector. As they sat by the crackling fire, she said, "Imagine living in California and having a fireplace. Needing a fireplace. I'm from New Orleans. I didn't normally associate California with fireplaces."

"California is a diverse place," he said. "It snows a lot in the Sierras. Down here in Carmel, people think of it as paradise: you know, Pebble Beach just a short ride away, Clint Eastwood was our mayor in the Eighties and so on. But it's horribly expensive here and the sun rarely shines. There's no home mail delivery, either. You have to go to the post office to get your letters. Is that really your idea of paradise?"

She shrugged. "I guess paradise is an internal thing that has nothing to do with houses or weather."

He nodded. "Exactly." Then, "Are you still concerned about going back to the radio station and having to deal with...that situation?"

She frowned. "Well, yes."

"But you know we're going to catch him? You have faith in our ability? *My* ability?"

Desirée looked away. "I suppose."

"I wonder," he said, "if sometimes you think I'm just a big dumb cop."

"I've never said any such thing."

"But you don't like cops in general," he said.

She nodded. "I don't like cops in general. But that's not your problem and any of your business."

He said, "I know all about it, anyway. I've gotten pretty handy with the computer at work. Desirée Justine Dupree is not the most common of names. You were easy enough to find on the Internet."

"Meaning...?"

"I've looked you up on LexisNexis, Google and other sources. You told me your parents were cops. Finding out about them was not the most difficult of tasks."

She thrust out her jaw, resenting how he had pried into the most private areas of her life, even if he had done so with the best of intentions. "So you whipped out your tin and started sticking your nose into my life and discovered that my parents had been killed."

"It's part of my job."

"And was it my parents' job to be gunned down in front of their home as their children slept?"

He shook his head. "I didn't say that."

Desirée took a sip of wine. "Well, I guess you know the details. My father was involved in the arrest of the Midnight Saints, a New Orleans street gang. The ones who got away threatened to kill him. Well, nothing happened for the longest time, so my parents just shrugged it off as a bunch of hot air from street punks. But then one night, as my father parked in front of our house and started unloading his truck, some Midnight Saints jumped him."

Harris nodded. He knew what followed but stayed silent.

"My mother looked out the window, saw what was happening and took out her service revolver and opened fire. She killed two of them and they killed her and my father before it was all over." She paused. "A big crackdown on gangs happened because of that incident, but my parents died in it. The department's brass praised them and all that, but the brass weren't orphaned. Monique and I were."

"Your parents knew the risks when they joined the force," Harris said. "I live with the same dangers myself. I've been threatened more times than I can remember."

"Then why don't you retire from the damn force and just spend the rest of your life down here?"

"Because," he said, "I like my job. I'll bet your parents did, too. They died doing something they enjoyed. Is that such a bad thing?"

"No, it's not such a bad thing and you have nothing to apologize for. But I'm not about to get involved in cops or anything else that has anything to do with police work, so don't be hitting on me anymore. Understand?"

"Nope."

"Excuse me?"

"You heard me. I said nope. We're well past the point of your not getting involved with a cop. We're involved, Desirée, and *you* made that choice as much as I did." He looked at her with dead seriousness. "The fact of the matter is that I'm in love with you. Surely you know that by now."

He saw the revulsion in her face, as if she wanted to vomit. Then it passed and she pretended her distaste hadn't flashed across her face.

"Isn't that nice," he muttered as he drained his wineglass. He then stared ahead, as if thinking of one thing to say, vetoing it, then coming up with a different idea and nixing that one, too.

"Love." Desirée rolled the word around in her mouth before speaking it as if believing that its pronunciation would provide insights into its essential characteristics. "How long have we known each other, Harris? I think you're mistaking love for infatuation."

"You think, you think, you think," he said. "You think for a living. Turn it off. Just feel."

"I feel..." Just how much was she willing to tell

him? Her eyes darted past him, around the room, as if her feelings—or at least the words that could best describe them—lay scattered there. "Scared. Exhilarated. Frustrated. I already have a lifetime's worth of regrets. The past decade has gone by too fast. Too fast! I was a little nobody from New Orleans and then the world discovered what I could do. My life became a blur: Chicago, Boston, San Francisco. I'm always being challenged and scrutinized. Finally, when Monique and I moved into that house and it seemed things were getting a little bit normal, that weirdo caller started hassling me. So, behind my back, my boss calls you and Christina, and now you're laying this heavy I-love-you rap on me."

He nodded. "I see. Well, that's a start. Feelings."

"I don't jump into bed with men just because I feel a certain amount of attraction to them."

"'A certain amount of attraction.' I'm so flattered. Tell you what, Miz Dez. Marry me and we can spend the next few decades exploring that 'certain amount of attraction.'"

"Ha, ha," she said, not smiling.

"No jokes here," he said, his eyes boring into hers. "We can drive up to Reno or Tahoe and do the deed. Think I'm kidding? I am not kidding. I don't kid about things like this."

She took a deep breath and looked around at the warm, comfortable room and the rich, handsome man who'd just propsed marriage and could offer her the whole world. "Harris, you're ludicrous."

"Love is never ludicrous." He pulled her closer. "I want you for myself for the rest of my life. I want all of you all the time. Say yes."

"Maybe." She freed herself from his grip and said, "No. I'm not marrying till I'm sure he's the right guy for me and I definitely don't think that marrying the cop who's trying to save me from the stalker is the right thing to do."

"You will marry some lucky man. That's

inevitable. What you have to do now is work on accepting the fact that the lucky man you're going to marry is me." He bent down and resumed kissing her neck.

"And make the same mistake twice?" she said. "No, thanks."

He jerked his head away from her neck and stared at her. "Don't ever mention your ex to me again, understand? You were a child who by mistake married some clown who didn't know the first thing about being a husband."

"Wasn't trying to compare you with anyone," she murmured, shocked by his sternness. "Divorce is done by two people. My fault as well as his."

"Then tell me this. When was the last time *this* happened to you?"

He grabbed and kissed her, nearly swallowing her whole. She felt overwhelmed and invaded, unable to draw breath.

In protest? In pleasure? Even she couldn't tell. Sensations swarmed trhough her like thousands of swirling stars, all heat and light. Before she could draw and release a breath, she was tossed into the storm.

No. Her mind all but screamed it. No one. Never. Only he had ever caused a hunger so sharp and a need so desperate. Even as her body strained against his, she struggled to remember that it wasn't enough to want. It wasn't always enough to have.

Whipped by fury and frustration, he crushed his mouth to hers again, again and yet again. If only for this moment, he would prove to her that what they had together was unique to them. She would think of no one, remembering nothing. Only him.

Her response tore through him, so complete, so right. The small, helpless sound that purred up through her throat shuddered into him. Like the flames that rose beside them, what they created burned and consumed. The gentle loving that had initiated them both during the night was replaced by a wildness she had experienced with no other man. They made love for what seemed an eternity, and then they slept. She had wonderful dreams which she could not remember in the morning.

...

Dressed in Harris's large crimson sweatshirt emblazoned with the faded words STANFORD UNIVERSITY, Desirée sat at the kitchen table and devoured Harris's spicy, piping-hot stew. Certain activities stimulated her appetite, and she had just finished one of them. Golden light and the glow of polished wood surrounded her. Outside she saw cypress trees and the calm Pacific Ocean. Even at her house in San Francisco, at her most serene moments, she had seldom felt this much at home. Her weekend was almost over; soon Kelvin would call her back to San Francisco, to resume her battle with the maniac who had been terrorizing her.

"You like?"

Desirée looked up to see Harris in a paisley robe and not much else. "I like," she said, not sure what she was admitting to liking. With him one couldn't be sure, and there were a number of things in that room at that moment she found most agreeable. She hoped he wasn't about to bring up marriage and commitment again. Sex made her hungry. She just wanted to eat.

"I meant, do you like the stew?" he asked.

She smiled and looked down at the bowl of savory brown broth that was brimming with large cubes of succulent beef and sweet, plump vegetables. A loaf of fresh sourdough bread lay next to it and there was a chilled bottle of Chablis to wash it all down. She giggled. "Wonderful."

"What's funny?"

"I was just thinking—"

"There you go, thinking again—"

"I was just thinking, not for the first time, how odd you are. You do so many things when you have more than enough money to live well for any number of lifetimes. You could hire people to do your cooking, cleaning and whatever else."

He sat down at the table. "Well, Mrs. Cavanaugh——"

"Who?" she snapped. "Mrs. Cavanaugh? Do I look like your mother?"

"You'll be the newest Mrs. Cavanaugh soon enough."

"Like hell."

He smirked, shoveling into his mouth a spoonful of stew. She had the sexiest damn voice he had ever heard. She sounded just as good in person as she did on the radio. She was also very much the same person on the air or off. Her success in broadcasting had been due just to that——being herself.

"Men always think women need them. That we can't have fulfilling, gratifying lives without some guy sharing our lives and beds." She paused. "That's just such an incredibly chauvinistic attitude men have."

"I don't recall saying any such thing. I simply

proposed marriage."

"But you implied that I needed you in order to have a fulfilling life——"

"I implied nothing. Maybe you're having flashbacks to your last experience with a man who wanted to marry you."

"My ex? I thought you didn't want me to bring him up ever again."

"You're right. Let's drop it."

"OK." She ate more stew.

"You should be flattered by my proposal. How many other men have asked you to marry them?"

She guffawed. "Are you kidding? I'm a foxy radio babe. I've been proposed to by men in four major cities."

He snarled. "You'd never even met them. You weren't in love with them."

"Oh, and am I in love with *you*?" she said with an

iciness she didn't feel.

"Ouch." He finished off his stew and said, "We both know how you feel about our relationship. Sooner or later you'll grow up and acknowledge those feelings."

Her eyes narrowed. "'Grow up'? *That* crap again?"

"If the shoe fits..."

She set down her spoon and stared at him. "Here is why I won't marry you. You're exactly the kind of person I trash on the radio: spoiled, cocky, pushy. You think you can have whatever and whoever you want, period."

"Oh, I think we'd make a dandy couple. I also think that once we parted company you would want me back in the worst way."

Desirée laughed. "You're worse than a radio groupie. We have them, too, just like rock stars. There was this guy in Boston who became obsessed with me. I made my share of personal appearances, and guess who was there at each one. He became sort of my one-man welcoming committee. He learned my birthdate and sent me flowers and Belgian chocolates." She shook her head and lit a cigarette. "He thought he was in love with me. Well, maybe he was. I thought he needed to get a life, real bad."

Harris frowned. He got up, went over to the kitchen counter, found a notepad and pen and sat back down, bemused. "What happened when you told him you were moving out to California?"

"I didn't actually tell him. I didn't even say goodbye to my listeners. I just ended my last show, left the studio and that was that."

Harris sat with the pen in hand, as if eager to start writing. "Do you remember his name? What he looked like?"

"He wasn't a big deal, Harris. Just some lonely young guy who decided I was the gal for him."

"So what was his name?" Harris asked again, twirling the pen between his fingers.

She closed her eyes and thought. Images, voices and sound bites swirled about in her head, comprising virtually her entire memory of those two years in Boston. Desirée, by the time she had become a prominent broadcasting personality, had learned one important lesson about playing the game: pay attention to those who could benefit her and ignore those who couldn't. It took her a few moments, but she managed to conjure up the name of the adoring fan whose identity Harris insisted on learning. "Clive? No, Michael. Michael...Saburn."

He wrote it down. "You didn't mention a Michael Saburn when I picked your brain earlier. Every lead is worth pursuing."

Desirée blew out a cloud of smoke. "Not worth mentioning. I repeat: he was some lonely guy who became interested in me. Michael was just this short, chubby redhead from Canada. He was about twenty-five and had just dropped out of Vancouver Community College. He worked under the table somewhere because he didn't have a green card and he had some stupid idea about attending Harvard eventually. He had a cell phone and a Walkman, so he would call me when I was on the air talking about something that interested him. He came to a couple of my personal appearnces and said hi. He wasn't the least bit dangerous, Harris."

"Everyone is potentially dangerous," he said. She could practically hear the clicking between his ears, the accumulation and classification of information. Harris the lover was now Inspector Cavanaugh, scribbling away on the pad at the top of which he had written, in bold block letters, MICHAEL SABURN.

*Every lead is worth pursuing. Everyone is potentially* dangerous. The words thundered in her ears. Desirée hated Harris for the moment. All his levity was gone. She wanted him to start teasing her again with marriage proposals——anything but this grim cop stuff. Could goofy, shy little Michael *really* have anything to do with the harassment she was experiencing at KCA?

"How long did you know him? I need to know

these things," Harris said.

"For the better part of a year. He came by my apartment building one evening and buzzed my suite," she remembered. "He wanted to come up for a cup of coffee. It really got Monique freaked. Like I said, I quit Boston and left without a trace. Figured I would never see him again."

Harris looked up at her. "Dez, this is the computer age. People can't just disappear. If Michael Saburn really wanted to know where you'd gone and the Boston station wouldn't tell him, he could just go online and track you down in five minutes."

"Well, the weirdo calling me now isn't Michael. Their voices are different."

"I didn't say they were the same person. Maybe Michael knows the weirdo caller and the weirdo caller thinks he's doing Michael a favor by hassling you. That would sort of explain things. After all, the caller keeps saying you killed someone he loved and he's going to get revenge."

Once again, she felt confused and afraid, thinking at first that it was absurd to suspect Michael Saburn of being anything but a little lost boy from her past, then suddenly seeing the logic in Harris' demanding to know Michael's full name and how long they had known each other. It really did seem to fit.

What did not fit was Harris' ancient Stanford sweatshirt. Desirée suddenly felt ridiculous sitting there in it. She took another sip of wine and swallowed hard.

Harris started clearing the table. "I don't have a computer down here, otherwise I would look into this right now," he said. "I really think we may be on to something here, Desirée. We're going back up to San Francisco tomorrow morning."

. . .

Desirée tossed and turned all night. Harris' dreams were a scramble of scenes in which he chased a man who at the last minute got away. Back in the city, another man slept poorly, too, but for somewhat different reasons.

He stared at the TV set, as always, but paid only occasional attention to the DVD of Charles Bronson in *Death Wish*. He thought about the woman on the radio, though she was not on the air. He knew she was with that cop and where they had probably gone. And what she was certainly doing with him at that moment. She was giving to that bastard what Michael would have happily given anything for. The man thought of her naked, in the cop's arms, giving him the most precious thing she had——herself.

But it would end. Soon.

He watched Bronson on the TV screen in his dark little apartment, smiled as he watched Bronson blow away the bad guys who had done him wrong. The man knew it was fake, of course, and that Bronson was just an actor who probably had never even fired a gun. But Desirée's mystery caller had shot and killed many men and knew it wasn't so hard. He had gone to war and done it. In fact, it was frequently downright easy, especially when you were doing the person——and the rest of the world——a favor by pulling the trigger or plunging the knife, and he had done it both ways in the jungle, many years earlier, and he had killed those people because Uncle Sam had sent him over to do just that. When the time came, and it would come very soon, he would be doing her a favor and certainly he would be giving Michael the greatest gift of all. that he and Michael would meet up again when the time came. Maybe he, Michael and the bitch could even become friends up there. This life would just be a trial for the next life, which would be so much better than anything he could ever imagine. But first, of course, he had some business to take care of here on Planet Earth, and he knew the pigs were after him. He needed to do it, and soon.

# CHAPTER 10

In downtown San Francisco, a brisk, fresh bay breeze blew clayey clouds across the sky. Harris loved such weather and might have even spent the day outside, but today he sat at his desk at the police station, his eyes glued to the computer screen. He wanted to know more about Michael Saburn.

At the moment, though, he was learning about Jim Yount, who did weekends on KCA. Yount and Desirée had worked together in Chicago, a fact that Desirée had for some reason withheld. Yount had become addicted to cocaine and his increasingly erratic behavior had cost him his job, while Desirée's stable behavior had gotten her Yount's job. He entered a treatment program and managed to overcome his addiction. Harris was surprised that KCA had taken a chance with the reformed Jim

Yount, even though doing weekends wasn't such a big chance.

"I don't seriously think that Jim Yount is behind this harassment case," said Christina Anchor as she swigged at a bottle of iced tea and handed Harris one. They took turns nibbling at the can of gourmet roasted cashews Harris had just opened. "He's too determined to get his life back together to risk doing time for threatening a colleague."

"Yeah, Yount is probably innocent," Harris said. "Who else we got?"

"Matt McDonald."

Harris frowned. "The gofer?"

"I believe the word is 'intern.'"

"Him? A suspect?" Harris asked.

"Maybe. He discreetly tries to get personal information from KCA staff about the Ragin' Cajun," she said. "I guess he's just too chickenshit to ask her out."

"That *is* pretty chickenshit," said Harris.

They both laughed. "He got pissed when he found out that the love of his life was divorced. I guess he had this fantasy about her being a sweet little virgin just like him."

Harris clucked. "Poor baby."

"I talked to Monique, too. She's much more forthcoming now. I looked her up online and stuck my nose into her personal stuff. Med school. Did you know she's number one in her class so far at U.C.S.F.?"

"She should become a psychiatrist. Once her male patients meet her, they'll forget all about the girlfriends who've dumped them."

"Monique thinks you and Desirée might have a future together."

"Monique is a very, very intelligent woman," said Harris.

Christina made a face. "I wonder if you are

261

making the right decisions in this case."

Harris eyed her. "Meaning what?"

"I mean your relationship with Desirée Dupree seems to be more than strictly professional."

"No comment."

"Just be sure our boss doesn't catch on. He would reassign you in a heartbeat."

Harris rolled his eyeballs. "Thanks, Mom."

"I'm serious. You know how hazardous it is to get emotionally involved with someone you're supposed to protect. As if this job isn't hazardous enough already."

"Well, Mom," he said in a voice implying that this subject was starting to annoy him, "if I start to think I'm in too deep, I'll give the Dupree file to someone else. And if I ever start to think I want to eat my handgun for dinner, I'll just find another line of work."

"Just so long as you do your thinking with the big

head"—she pointed at his lap—"and not the little head."

He rolled his eyeballs. "Thanks for worrying about my two heads, Mom."

She sat on his desk and stared down at him. "Seriously, Harris, we've known each other for a little while now, right? I don't want to see you get in over your head and end up with huge psychiatric problems. This woman, Dupree, is very charismatic. Men find her voice really sexy. And the fact that she seems to be stubbornly single makes her that much more desirable. But you? Hell, you're talking about *marrying* her. What's up with that?" Christina shook her head. "There's something not quite right about her. Something dangerous."

"Danger is my business," Harris deadpanned, not for the first time. Translation: shut up about my relationship with Desirée.

"Whatever," said Christina. "The harassment doesn't appear to be an inside job. All those KCA employees seem to have normal, stable lives and no obvious cause for making those calls to Dupree." She paused. "All in all, a nice enough bunch of people who all seem to respect each other."

"They don't even seem to mind it when the Ragin' Cajun gets on the air and starts assassinating their values," said Harris.

Christina offered him a small, derisive smile. "I know. I listen to her on the radio as she rags on everyone—the CIA, the IRS, the FBI, everyone on Capitol Hill and beyond. Then she gets into that little BMW and drives home to her big-ass house. Western Broadcasting pays her more than most of her audience makes. Doesn't she realize that she's exploiting the very system she wants to destroy?"

"Maybe just a tiny bit," Harris replied. "Deep down, she knows she's just talking the talk. Nothing she says makes a damn bit of difference."

"Except to KCA's sales department, where they can hike up commercial rates because the Cajun has the best ratings around," Christina noted. "So, what do we know about this Michael Saburn?" she added.

"Boston said they would get back to me." Then, "Last person on the KCA list is Jimmy Meyer, the electrician. Vietnam veteran, honorable discharge May 1975. One of those guys...what do the shrinks call it? Post-traumatic Stress Disorder. Guy has had some trouble staying put since coming home. Lived in a dozen states. Came from a broken home."

"Now he's changing lightbulbs at Broadcast House. Difficult road he's traveled."

"We'll wait and see about Saburn in Boston. Nobody at KCA seems to represent any leads," said Harris.

Just then the phone rang. He picked it up. "Cavanaugh. Boston? Good. I've been awaiting your call." His face darkened and he grabbed his pad of Post-It notes and started with his own unique shorthand that only he could read. "Thanks." He hung up the phone.

"So…?"

"Boston says Michael Saburn committed suicide last year. Shot himself in the head. Guess what the autopsy report says he had tattooed on his arm?"

"What?"

"Desirée."

"Well," Christina muttered, "*that* helps."

…

Desirée Dupree would not have called herself a religious woman, but she prayed, to a God in whom she did not believe, that somewhere in Boston, Michael Saburn was alive and well. Better still, that Michael was back home in Vancouver, taking creative-writing courses at Vancouver Community College.

When her phone rang, she was eager for good news and a reassuring voice. "Harris…?"

*"Did you fuck him? Did you suck his cock? Did he come in your face?"*

She struggled to swallow. Gasping, she asked, "Who wants to know?"

"Did he fuck you in the ass? Did you like it? Did you want him to do it again?" His infernal laughter screamed into her ears.

"Go...away...please."

"The cop got what he wanted. He got what you would never give to the best friend you never had." Pause. "The cop will get more than what he wanted. You will die for this and so will that pig you fucked."

"So why haven't you——"

"Killed you yet? Time is coming soon, bitch. You and the pig." Click.

Desirée's mind and heart raced. She was in her T-shirt and jeans, in the comfort of her home, with the cops and their resources on her side, the nightmare refused to go away. The caller wanted her and Harris to die. A confrontation seemed inevitable and people would die. She wanted to warn Harris to be careful, although a man in his profession hardly needed to hear such advice. Somehow, though, Desirée felt convinced that this telephone terrorist was a far more dangerous adversary than any police officer was prepared for.

Just then the doorbell rang. She sprinted over and opened it without looking through the peephole.

"Matt?" She wasn't sure if she was relieved or disappointed. She knew he would prolong this visit as much as possible. He always did.

"Right." The intern looked her up and down. "You look all shaken up."

"The guy just called again. Said he was going to kill me and Harris. I've got to tell him what's going on before this maniac gets to him."

"You think that six-foot-something cop with the big gun under his coat is afraid of some jerk-off out there?"

Desirée was taken aback by his directness. "What's that supposed to mean?"

"It means that you shacked up with him. I know you did." Matt's voice cracked with emotion.

Desirée, instinctively resentful of having her personal life pried into, restrained herself from telling him off as she noticed the tears welling up in his eyes. She looked past him and saw his secondhand economy car parked at the curb. Had he come all this way just to accuse her of cheating on him...?

"Look, Matt, this is the worst possible time. Let's talk later, OK?"

He shook his head. "There's no later. My internship has ended. I just came to say thanks for your help."

"What help did I give you?"

"You made me believe in love," he said simply.

"You need to be with someone your own age," she told him. "I'm not the one for you, even though I may seem to be."

"You pretended that I didn't exist, or that I was

269

just some dumb flunky, and then that cop just stepped right in and helped himself to you, simple as you please. So now the cops want to talk to *me* about you to find out if I'm the guy who's been threatening you on the phone. Nice, huh?"

With that, he turned around and hurried down the stairs. He climbed into his car that wheezed and struggled away.

...

Desirée had to admit that San Francisco did sleaze as stylishly as it did everything else. She'd been to Times Square prior to its gentrification and nobody could have topped that neighborhood for funk and decadence. But San Francisco's Tenderloin, in places, was still a pretty down-and-dirty place. She stopped at 550 Golden Gate Avenue, her current employer's former location. The faded KCA logo was still prominent on the unoccupied building's front door. Street people milled past. Desirée tried not to notice as a black man urinated against the side of a building. She peered through a crusty window into the street-level broadcast booth from which John Granville, the station's morning host for three decades, had done his show throughout the 1970s. KCA was the only station anyone knew where the broadcast booth was visible from the street and passersby could stand and watch the talking heads. In 1973, one such passerby, a schizophrenic heroin addict, decided to liven things up a bit by pointing a .32 automatic at Granville and pumping two slugs at the revered broadcaster. Desirée had heard the tape of Granville's startled but largely controlled reaction. "Hey! I think someone just fired a shot at me!" There was no shortage of witnesses, and within minutes police chased the gunman into an alley where he fatally shot himself.

The station downplayed the incident and even replaced the window, in which were now embedded the two oval-shaped, brownish-looking bullets that had been destined for John Granville's revered head. The event revived the station's demands on its parent, Western Broadcasting, for offices and studios in a better part of town. Not an easy task.

Broadcasting facilities were special-needs children; the building could be neither too short or too tall; it would need to be outfitted with certain kinds of high-tech equipment. Simply buying another building was out of the question unless it had once been a radio or TV station. And, perhaps most important, the building had to be located in a safe, picturesque area where KCA's account executives could proudly take clients.

Western did not have the money for what KCA needed, but its parent, the behemoth cinema chain International Megaplex, did, so the suits back east transferred cash from one account into another and KCA went shopping for a new home. Western Broadcasting bought a parcel of land near the Financial District, removed whatever had been there and erected Broadcast House, which, Desirée Dupree agreed, was more than a tiny bit better than the old place in the Tenderloin.

Desirée observed, as she walked along Turk Street to the police station where Harris worked, that San Francisco was a city prone to dramatic changes. She had read books about the city's transformation as the powers-that-were invaded South of Market and the Tenderloin in the name of progress and turned much of it into an extension of the Financial District. Gone were the old but habitable weekly hotels that were many old people's homes. Justin Herman, namesake of the plaza near Powell Street, whom she had reviled more than once on the air even though he had died in 1971, had done a fine job of falsely promising displaced people with alternative, affordable housing and clearing the land for the Yerba Buena Center, Moscone Center and PacBell Park. Many of the bars and porn shops were gone, too, replaced by Starbuck's and Gap stores. Desirée thought it was probably inevitable. A city like San Francisco, with its worldwide appeal, couldn't have—or, as the redevelopers liked to say, didn't need--a skid row forever.

She stopped at her destination and stared for a moment at the imposing stone building whose front door bore the large gold letters SFPD. It looked nothing like any police station she had ever seen.

Back when the neighborhood was a viable commercial area, a handful of such buildings sprang up, invariably becoming banks or government buildings. As the area declined, the banks moved out. Needing a Tenderloin precinct, the San Francisco Police Department acquired this big, ornate building although it was too spacious for their purposes.

Desirée entered this building, where the normal turmoil of a police station was concealed. She had heard about the night, several years earlier, when a member of the Crips entered the station with a .44 Magnum revolver in his Raiders warmup jacket. The cop at the desk was too busy with paperwork to notice when the Crip withdrew the gun and blew most of the man's head off. The gangster then sauntered out and remained unidentified.

Thereafter, the officers of the Tenderloin precinct received the public from behind several inches of bulletproof glass, communicating through an audio system that made citizens feel as if the cop were talking to them from somewhere on Mars.

Desirée passed through the four-inch-thick metal door with its electronic bolt and encountered virtual sterility, as if being in a life-insurance office, with the insanity of the Tenderloin now just a memory. Different, she thought, how different from the environment her parents worked in back in New Orleans. She remembered the lineoleum and grime, the stink of stale coffee. But here were gleaming computers, carpeted floors and plainclothes cops who looked as if they'd get around to solving cases whenever they felt like it.

She spotted Harris as he emerged from an interrogation room. Behind him were Jim Yount and Christina Anchor. Yount saw her and waved. Then the three of them approached Desirée.

"Jimbo," she said, "what's going on?"

Yount shrugged. "The usual. Being interrogated by the cops over some bullshit harassment issue." He laughed. "Not me. I'm not *the* weirdo, just *a* weirdo."

"Just so long as they understand the distinction," she said. "Wait a few minutes and I'll buy you a cup of coffee."

"Maybe next time," he said. "I'm due elsewhere."

"You're free to go, Mr. Yount," said Harris. A uniformed officer joined them to escort Yount through the station.

"You didn't think *he* was the one...?" Desirée said to Harris.

"*Everyone* is a potential suspect," he replied.

"So you've said. I'd have vouched for Yount."

"You're right, he's not our guy," Harris said. "So, what brings you to the Tenderloin? What's on your mind?"

"A word with you in private. In there." She pointed to the room in which Harris and Christina had just questioned Yount.

Harris shrugged "OK."

They went inside and as soon as Harris closed the door, Desirée asked, her manner slow and careful, as if diplomacy at this instant were paramount, "Mind if

I ask why you had Jim in here?"

"Because you two worked together back east. He was a cocaine addict and got fired. You took over his job. So you meet up again here. Maybe there's some lingering resentment. We had to check it out."

"Well, he's had some difficult times and made some bad decisions. He's been straight for a few years now and goes to support-group meetings. When he keeps dope out of his nose, he's a highly stable individual."

"And when he keeps dope *in* his nose, he's volatile as all hell, according to employment and police records," Harris pointed out.

"Well, then, let's hope he keeps the dope out of his nose for good." She paused. "But enough about him. I got another threatening call on my home phone."

He just nodded.

Desirée swallowed hard. "He said he was going to kill *you*, too."

"So what? We've had your home phone hooked up for tracing. Remember? The call you just got came from the same bank of Fisherman's Wharf phones that he's used before."

"Aren't you alarmed that he's after *you*, too?"

Harris gave a small, bitter laugh. "He's been after my ass since I was assigned to protect you. In fact, half the Crips and Bloods in the Bay Area would like to feed me my own scrotum for breakfast."

Desirée cringed. "Still——"

"No ifs, and, buts or stills. You're being harassed. We're the cops on your case. We catch the perp and you get on with your life. Period."

Desirée swung around and faced Christina. "So what do *you* have to say about all this? Wanna know something? I have a personal relationship with Harris. Did he tell you I fucked his brains out down in Carmel——"

Christina looked away.

"Desirée," Harris said. "You can do whatever you want. You can go to my boss and insist on having me, or both of us, replaced. He'll probably do that, too, but it won't do a damned bit of good. If anyone's going to catch the caller, it will be us. We have the most experience after being on this case. Do what you think is best."

Desirée sighed, unable to argue with sound logic. Harris was right. He and Anchor needed to stay on the case. It would be pointless to bring in someone new. In a voice slightly above a whisper, she said, "I just couldn't handle it...if something happened to you."

He offered her the cockiest of smiles. "As I like to say, 'Danger is my business.'"

"Don't get smug with me. I don't think I could stand it to have anything happen to you."

"I'm just telling you how it is. Nobody scares me. I couldn't function in my job if I had fear to deal with all the time." He pulled out a file and showed it to her. "There will be no better time to deal with *this* matter."

"What's that?"

"Michael Saburn."

Desirée raised her eyebrows in surprise. "You tracked him down. I hope he's back home in Canada, married with a kid on the way."

"Nope. Dead and buried."

She shook her head. "Impossible. Maybe it's a different Michael Saburn."

"The same one. About half a year ago."

She sighed, then rested her head in her hands. "Unreal. Everything that's happened. And now this. Michael said he might do something desperate, but people say that all the time and they don't actually..."

"Sometimes they do attempt suicide," Harris said. "And sometimes they succeed." He paused. "Plus, he had a long psychiatric history. Despite having no green card, he moved from Canada to Boston with some notion about studying creative writing at

Harvard. At first he was OK, so long as his little bubbles weren't being burst."

"He was so gentle and vulnerable," Desirée remembered.

"So he got fixated on you, this radio babe who rejected him and things really started going downhill." Harris offered her an ironic grin. "There's nothing like a taste of real life to mess up a good fantasy."

"I was mean to him. I should have been more of a friend," she said.

"Nonsense," Harris said. "He just would have taken you down with him. He was bad news."

"Easy for *you* to say that. You don't have to cope with the pressures of public life the way I do."

"Oh, don't I? Gee, I guess I keep forgetting what an easy and safe little job I have." Then, "Right now, my job is to figure out what Michael Saburn might have to do with the guy who's been threatening you over the phone. The caller always says, 'You killed the best friend I ever had.' Now I need to figure out which of Saburn's buddies came out here to harass you. Tell me again what you remember."

She closed here eyes and went through it all over again. "I had fans there in Boston, you know. Not just him. Lots of them saw me as some kind of potential girlfriend. To me it was all just PR and promotion, part of the job. They show up where I'm doing something live, I say hello, we visit for a moment or two and it's like I gave them something to take home with them, a souvenir. They stay fans indefinitely. It's good for business. Some of them don't have anything better to do than call me on a regular basis. Like Michael. Then he started up with the cards and candy. Again, some guy out there with lots of time on his hands. At the station they laughed about it. But then, when he showed up at my apartment and buzzed me! How did he get my address? Did he follow me home or something? Damn." She sighed. "So he can't have me and kills himself, and now his pal has moved out here and starts hassling me on the phone."

"That's showbiz," Harris said.

"Ha, ha." Then, "For me, the final straw was the last time we saw each other. He rolled up his sleeve and showed me this awful tattoo of my name. I told him I thought it was juvenile for him to disfigure his arm that way."

"And how did he feel about that?"

Desirée's eyes grew wide. "Oh, he got pissed. Real pissed. Said he'd done it to honor me and that his dad actually gave him the tattoo in the first place."

"His dad was in Boston with him?"

Desirée shrugged.

Harris shook his head. "His father died when Saburn was a child."

Desirée threw out her arms. "Well, there was *someone* he called 'Dad.'"

Harris opened Saburn's file and stared at it as if it

contained the secrets of the universe. "Dad is an older man who befriended a Canadian misfit. The misfit falls in love with a radio personality and is rejected. Dad swears vengeance, notices the woman is gone and tracks her down online. She's out here now, so he uproots himself and travels three thousand miles to give her some payback." Harris stroked his chin, convinced that the pieces had fallen perfectly into place. "Now the only question is: Who's Dad?"

"And let's hope we find Dad before he finds me," Desirée said.

# CHAPTER 11

The two Tylenol 3s barely eased Desirée's headache as she drove back home. The world's greatest control freak had watched her world go mad. Her relationship with Harris, her front-door confrontation with Matt McDonald, the knowledge that Michael Saburn had committed suicide and that his friend was almost certainly the harassing caller. She just wanted to get home, crawl into bed and never face the world again.

Desirée corrected herself. She wanted to take her life back. She wanted enough peace and quiet to figure out how to fix her own problems. She had thrived in a brutal profession because of her toughness and tenacity. Now was not the time to back down and run away. When had she ever lacked nerve or courage? And why did she feel that she was in this all alone? The cops were involved and were getting closer to nailing the caller. She tried to imagine who he might be. A middle-aged man, angry but clever, someone who knew how to harass and kill. Someone who had access to her, who had been wily enough to obtain her home and work addresses. She knew of no one. She wondered if, unknowingly, she had actually looked into the man's eyes—into a killer's eyes, the eyes of the man planning to kill her—and seen only kindness and friendship.

She looked in the rearview mirror and saw Harris tailing her in his charcoal-gray Aries. She didn't really want to have him around for the rest of the day but was too fatigued to argue with him, so she stayed silent as they left the Tenderloin police station, got their cars and began the long, slow drive to Juanita Way.

Once she reached home, she eased into her garage as Harris parked at the curb. Soon she let him in and they were both in her living room. He sat on her huge sofa while she looked out the window and saw yet another impossibly gray San Francisco sky. She started blaming her problems on the city that she now lived in. No wonder the previous owner of her home had sold the place to her. How difficult it was to maintain any sense of optimism about life when outside it was so often gray! She had read about Alaska and Sweden, two places so far north that the lack of wintertime sunlight induced periods of depression. Well, San Francisco, she told herself, could do a pretty good job of grinding people down, too.

She wished some program director in Honolulu would tune in some night, fall in love with the Ragin' Cajun and offer her a job in the Aloha State. You couldn't stay depressed for long when the weather was so beautiful. She could get a suntan. She could learn to surf. She had always meant to try riding the waves.

"Hungry?" he asked.

"Not much." She stared outside at the Victorian homes much like her own, the smart imported cars parked everywhere. It all seemed so foreign to her now, as if she were living in some European country.

"I'm sure Monique bought some stuff and put it in the icebox if you want something to eat."

Harris got up and stood behind her. "Sleepy?"

"Last thing on my mind." Then, "Doesn't this weather get you down? Always gray and awful. I'm surprised people here aren't jumping out of their windows every day."

"Not the weather that's getting to you, kiddo. It's...other things. Once this shit storm has passed, San Francisco will start looking pretty damn sexy again."

"Baseball season starts soon," she murmured. "That always cheers me up."

Harris put his arms around her. "We'll get season's tickets to watch the Giants. When they have the day off, we'll take BART across the Bay and watch the A's. We'll spend the summer at the ballparks, eating hot dogs and drinking beer. Sound like a plan?"

"Best offer I've gotten lately." She smiled at the warmth of his arms around her. "I was lying about this house and city. It's mine. It says so on the deed. For the past decade I've been hopping from city to city. Hotels or apartments, because I didn't know how long I would be there till a better job came along. When my boss here called and wanted to offer me a spot at KCA, I think Monique and I were just starting to get used to Boston. Imagine a couple of Dixie chicks in New England. We stayed just long enough for her to graduate from Boston University. I hope she feels at home here and graduates at the top of her class and stays a long time."

"Maybe all of this was meant to be. You and her in San Francisco. And you here with me, right now."

"I remember what I said on the air about San Francisco. It's so crazy and progressive and fascinating. I guess I meant all those things."

"Sounds like you're going native," Harris said.

"All this time it's been Monique and me, period. I didn't think there was room for one more in my life. Anyway, I didn't think I would find a partner. I figured Monique would fall in love with some hunk and move in with him, and I would be, as the song says, 'Alone again, naturally.'"

"It doesn't have to be that way and you know it," he said, putting the gentlest kiss on her lips.

"No," she said, with the smallest shake of her head. "There you go again, refusing to listen."

"Oh, I'm listening," he murmured. "I'm just expressing the opposing viewpoint."

"I'm not asking to you agree with me. I just want you to accept what can't be changed."

"Most things in the world can be changed. Most things can be improved." He continued, "Once this ordeal is over, you and I should have a nice long visit about life, love and happiness."

"When this nightmare is over," she said, suddenly grim, "one of us may not survive to have that visit. So, I'm wondering: were you kidding me about getting married?"

"I'm never kidding about marriage."

"So we'll elope in Reno tonight, do the deed and live happily ever after. Your family is rich. We'll both retire and spend the rest of our lives down in Carmel." She grinned at him and used his favorite expression. "Sound like a plan?"

His face darkened. "Not funny, Dupree."

She cocked an eyebrow. "Am I laughing, Cavanaugh?"

"I'm trying to have a very serious conversation with you."

"They're the best kind."

"Marriage is not a bargaining tool. 'I'll marry you if you'll get off the case and hide in Reno like a little asshole because I don't think you're a good enough cop to catch the bad guy *and* stay alive.'"

She shook her head. "I didn't say any such thing. But he was just so menacing on the phone today. He's fucking deranged. He's bent on wasting us both."

"So we'll get him before that happens. We do it all the time. It's what we get paid for."

...

Desirée tried to pretend it was just another night at work as she sat in the studio. She sat at the microphone, giddy, mellow, passive, her finger nowhere near the mute button. Each caller spoke his mind, largely about local politics. She listened, asked a polite question or two and moved on until Jay gave her the sign of an imminent break.

The red light went out and Desirée dragged on a cigarette.

"Tonight you're not ragin', Cajun," Harris murmured from his corner by the window.

"Tonight they're getting the kinder, gentler Desirée."

"Bad idea. You're here to kick some ass." He had to fly to Los Angeles for some professional function the next morning—maybe Taser had made a new kind of stun gun that offered more zapping power.

Desirée hoped his business would keep him down there for a week, at least. Maybe in Harris's absence, the harassing caller, through with phone calls and ready to fulfill his threats, would pounce on her in Broadcast House's parkade and be blown away by Christina Anchor.

Whatever would happen, would happen. She just didn't want it happening to Harris. If a fatal confrontation happened, she wanted it to be between Christina and the maniac in a shootout. The cop would get a heroine's burial and Desirée would get Harris.

Broadcast House was locked up for the night. The security guards loitered in the lobby. So far as Desirée could tell, only she, Jay and Harris remained on KCA's floor.

"Midnight is just two hours away," Harris pointed out. "Want to come home with me? We can cuddle up and play Trivial Pursuit."

"I'll consider it if you pass my little quiz," she said.

He sighed. "Talk."

"What does G.O.P. stand for?"

He laughed. "Is that the best you can do? It's the Grand Old Party, ma'am."

"Which president served the longest?"

He sighed. "F.D.R. He died in office."

"Name the capital of Missouri," she said.

"Got me on that one. I know it isn't St. Louis or Kansas City. Is it? Shit, man, I give up."

"Jefferson City."

"You sure about that? Is there a computer around here? I want to check this out."

"Take my word for it." She stretched and suddenly found herself almost unable to stay awake. She blinked repeatedly. "First I can't sleep, then I can't stay awake at work."

"Coffee time." Harris slipped out of the broadcast booth and headed down the deserted hallway, his heels clicking on the gleaming parquet floor. He liked Broadcast House when that stuck-up asshole Kelvin Barrow was gone, along with the army of others who occupied KCA during business hours. Actually, he liked that workaholic intern, Matt McDonald, who always used to make fresh, hot coffee. But Matt had quit impulsively after putting two and two together about Desirée's new relationship. As Harris ripped open a fresh package of coffee in KCA's designer-decorated kitchen, he predicted Matt would soon miss this fancy-ass place and all the people he admired. Harris imagined hearing Matt carry on, if only in private, about Desirée: "She's fucking him! She's fucking that big cop!"

He empathized with the youngster, watching the coffee drip into the pot. *Happens to the best of 'em, Matt. Don't take it so hard. It's no fun being 20 years old and in love with——or at least horny as hell for——a 28-year-old you can't have. You need a girlfriend your own age, the sooner the better. You just aren't Desirée's type. I should know because I am her type and I have the damnedest time figuring her out.*

He made Desirée a cup of coffee and decided against making a brief check of the floor. He was sure it was just himself, Desirée and Jay. The other radio station downstairs would have only a couple of people, too, and the TV station would be at minimal staff. A few security guards would be downstairs. Harris occasionally wondered if Broadcast House had a ton of gold bullion stashed somewhere; security at that building was a top priority. At the Federal Building at the Civic Center they seemed less paranoid than these media people did.

Harris was grateful that the Boston authorities had gotten back to him so quickly about Michael Saburn. That was the break he had needed. Saburn's "dad" was the caller, a damned clever guy who had eluded the cops thus far. But Harris knew he and the caller would soon meet soon. He just hoped the arrest happened before the blood spilled.

The break ended and he heard Desirée through the kitchen speakers. That voice. Magic. How long had he been hearing it? Since forever yet not long enough. Often he scarcely heard what she said; it was enough just to hear the low purr coming from her throat.

Matt McDonald Michael Saburn, Harris Cavanaugh—no man could help falling in love with her. She was simply irresistible.

He smelled the delightful aroma of fresh coffee and glanced with appreciation at the foil package he had just emptied. Gourmet blend, yummy stuff. At least KCA didn't skimp on its java. You got what you paid for in this life, that was for damned sure. Desirée needed this caffeine rush. He wanted to do his thing in Los Angeles as fast as possible, then get back to San Francisco and nail the weirdo who was harassing his woman.

Just then he heard some sort of disturbance out in the hallway. He felt sure it wasn't anything but checked just the same.

"It's closing in on midnight." Desirée's lovely voice caressed his ears through the ceiling's speakers as Harris, gun drawn, crept towards the broadcast booth. He cursed the parquet floor that announced his every step. The storage room was just a few steps away, to his right. His heart started pounding; something was amiss.

"Manny Ramirez will be in after the local news. We still have a few lines open and our number is 800-555-2KCA."

Harris breathed a bit easier. The place was safe. He was jumpy. The problem was his imagination. He didn't hear the gentle click of the storage-room door any more than he heard the muffled shot that brought him down.

"I'm Desirée Dupree, the Ragin' Cajun on KCA, Newstalk Radio Nine-eighty."

Desirée heard the rah-bum-bum of the national news intro and took off her headphones. Why was Harris taking so long with the coffee? She got up and walked over to the door and saw that half the hallway was inexplicably dark. Her heart froze.

She stepped out into the hallway and smiled,

clutching her chest. She spotted a familiar figure in the darkness and smiled. "Whew! It's only you. I thought we were all alone up here."

"Yes. We are alone. There's nobody else." The man stepped closer, into the light. Desirée stopped smiling. She could now see the .45 automatic in his hand.

"Harris...?" she asked, swallowing hard.

"You don't want to know about Harris."

There was nowhere to run. The unthinkable yet inevitable confrontation was now happening. She looked at the man's face for the longest instant, then stared at his gun. She spoke his name, as she had done a hundred times.

"Jimmy."

The Gentle Electrician. Mr. Nice Guy. Mr. Fixit. Arguably the only person at Broadcast House who could travel unquestioned anywhere within the building. He was wearing his usual green uniform with the oval name patch. The only difference now was that his toolbelt was gone. Now the only tool he needed was in his hand.

He smiled. "Yes, ma'am. It was me all along. Fooled ya, didn't I?"

He lunged at her and in a heartbeat had her in a headlock. He dragged her back inside the broadcast booth and pointed the gun's sight into her temple, his arms filled with iron determination.

"You killed my son," he said.

"He killed himself," she said in a tiny voice. "I didn't even know him..."

"He was in love with you," Jimmy said, his voice still soft and free of anger. "You would have loved him. You could have learned to love him."

He adjusted the gun and fired a shot so that the bullet grazed Desirée's temple. Cold panic seized her.

"The most beautiful man alive gave you his heart and you rejected him," Jimmy said.

"He was confused. He didn't know what he wanted." Desirée's head spun. She was simply repeating what she had told herself so many times lately.

"He wanted you. You threw him away like trash. You were on such an ego trip that a humble, special young man like him was of no use to you." He fired another shot that whizzed past Desirée's face and thudded into the ceiling.

She whimpered and licked her lips. Jay was in the control booth, doubtless aware of the situation and wisely hiding. He had certainly called the cops. They would be here soon. But soon enough?

"He shouldn't have done it," she croaked. "He was a nice kid. If he had stayed around longer, he would have met someone who deserved him."

"He deserved to get whatever or whoever he wanted," Jimmy said. "He wanted you, so he should have gotten you." Another bullet flew past Desirée's head. She closed her eyes as tears streamed down her face.

"If you want to kill me," she managed to say, "there's not much stopping you now. But just tell me what happened to Harris."

"I already told you. I offed him. He's with Michael now. Or maybe he's burning in hell." Jimmy let out a maniacal laugh.

"Kill me too! Do it! Kill me!" she demanded.

"Fucking right. But his death was quick and painless. I'm gonna make you suffer for what you've done."

She could barely breathe from the tightness of his grip around her neck. Her ears rang from the two gunshots that had exploded a fraction of an inch from her temple. Then she realized her ears weren't ringing at all—she was hearing the sound of police sirens from just outside Broadcast House.

He threw her down and, nearly shaking with rage, pointed the gun at her. "I've been waiting for this moment for so long." His voice was just above a whisper. "I was going to make it last and make you suffer more, but I think I'll just kill you now."

Just then there was a hellish explosion of glass as the booth's door shattered. Desirée turned to see Harris standing in the hallway, pointing his weapon at Jimmy. The mystery caller tried to return fire but the cop shot again, sending Jimmy reeling past Desirée, his gun dropping by her side as he collapsed at the other end of the room.

Desirée struggled to her feet and, as if dreaming, saw Harris standing, unsteady, as Christina Anchor hurried up from behind him.

Rushing over to him, Desirée, insanely, tried to embrace him. Christina pulled her away.

"He's shot," Desirée said, her voice nearly inaudible. "Bad."

The woman cop nodded. "Ambulance is on its way. Don't touch him."

"Don't let him die," Desirée begged.

"Never," said Christina. "Not ever."

# CHAPTER 12

KCA was immediately filled with the usual chaos of a crime scene. Within minutes the radio station was filled with official-looking people wearing windbreakers as Jay, before exiting the control booth, pressed a button or two and an old Ragin' Cajun broadcast played for whomever was listening. The wounded man and dead man had both been driven away, to different places. Desirée and Christina got into the cop's unmarked cruiser; the car's flashing lights and siren made little impression on motorists they encountered as they hurried towards St. Jude, the nearest hospital, which was not very near at all.

By the time they reached the emergency room, hospital staff said only that Harris was in surgery. Desirée pictured doctors and nurses, raised voices, beeping machines, adrenalin pounding. All of that had happened minutes earlier, now behind double doors. Desirée assumed that the police department might know something but she and Christina could find nobody in a blue uniform, nobody official who could, or would, say if he was still alive.

Somebody dead, somebody wounded, somebody terrified but unharmed except for the shattered nerves, the crisis that had been started with mysterious phone calls, and soon known to all, had culminated in a shootout. The sensational news reports would follow: KCA mystery caller unmasked. The electrician. He had shot the cop. The cop had shot back, killing the bad guy. The cop was now, as the journalists liked to say, clinging to life.

Monique called from campus, demanding to know Harris's status. She then announced she was driving to the hospital whether she was needed there or not. The medical student, minutes later, marched into the waiting room and embraced her sister.

"Only the doctors and God know what's going on back there," said Desirée. "We were just getting used to each other, thinking, 'We may have a future together.' And now—"

"He ain't dead yet, Sis."

"He was all covered in blood. He'd lost so much."

"But now he's in surgery. And please don't blame yourself for any of this ugliness. OK?"

"I try never to place blame on anyone," she said. "I don't do that."

"Except on yourself," said Monique.

"And I wouldn't follow his orders. I made things difficult for him."

"You were no worse than many of his other assignments. And in many ways you were much better," said Christina. "Anyway, I'm sure he'll pull through. He couldn't possibly allow a world to exist that didn't include him." She pointed to a nearby bank of vending machines. "Coffee, anyone?"

The Dupree sisters nodded and Christina went over to the coffee machine, Monique following.

"Well, I think I'm sort of glad that this nightmare has played itself out," Monique said, sticking her debit card into the machine. She shuddered. "Imagine, the damn electrician."

"Yeah. Sneaky little bastard."

"I hope this experience won't warp my sister's future."

Christina shook her head. "It won't. The trauma usually doesn't linger for that long."

"Tell that to *her*."

"Maybe I should do exactly that." Christina had difficulty speaking to Desirée. A strange, indefinable competition existed between them, at least in her mind. Christina knew the other woman's powers, especially over Harris, whom they both adored. They seemed rivals for Harris's affections, and Christina, in ways that made her feel ashamed, blamed Desirée for being a special sort of person in life, the kind of individual who could captivate a million unseen strangers just with her voice and wits, and who could become the obsession of someone like Harris Cavanaugh, who Christina believed could have whichever woman he wanted. She also blamed Desirée for being the type of woman who, despite not wanting to do so, could effect a fatal confrontation between a deranged man and the one brought in to protect her.

Christina accepted two cups of coffee, sniffed them with distaste—she considered vending-machine coffee seldom worth drinking—and brought one over to Desirée. "Have some."

"Yummy," Desirée drawled, accepting the cup of muddy liquid with little enthusiasm. "I wonder if this"—she meant Harris's surgery—"should be done by now."

"The longer, the better," said Christina. "It means they've stabilized him. These things can take forever and a day. Sometimes they're as difficult for the surgeon as the patient."

"Let's hope you're right."

"I *am* right. I'm paid to be right," the police inspector said with the briefest of smiles.

"I guess you know that he and I started having a personal relationship because of all this. I just want you to know that it wasn't my idea to have things turn out this way. I would have taken the bullet—"

Christina put up a hand. "No, you're wrong. You *wouldn't* have taken the bullet. You didn't want to get shot, and that's why you let us watch your back. That was his job and mine too. We in police work confront danger all the time. We go looking for it, literally. He knew the risks associated with entering your life as a cop and as a man. He accepted those risks.

"Your engineer, Jay, called us while this was going on. Did you know that? We would have gotten there anyway, but he called us and we got there sooner. There *are* a few heroes in all this ugliness."

"Still, I want to blame someone for all this."

"There are three hundred million people in this

country. Blame every one of us because we all created Jimmy Lee Smith and Michael Saburn. Same society created Charles Manson, Juan Corona, Richard Ramirez, John Wayne Gacy and Jeffrey Dahmer. Nobody did much to help Jimmy Smith when he got back home from Vietnam. Michael Saburn came along and gave him a purpose in life, but Michael had a few problems of his own and Jimmy assumed Michael's problems. One unstable character makes friends with another and real life delivers a few wallops to them both and they can't handle it. One kills himself because the woman on the radio doesn't want him and his friend swears vengeance and almost kills the radio woman before a cop kills him." She sighed. "Never a dull moment here in these Yoo-nited States. Shit, I've been listening to you for so long that I'm starting to sound like the Ragin' Cajun!"

They both laughed. Then a man in fresh surgical greens came in and said, "Is the family of Harris Cavanaugh here?"

Desirée said, "This lady is his partner, Inspector

Anchor. The other one is my sister. What about Inspector Cavanaugh?"

The doctor, probably the surgeon who had just operated on Harris, seemed as nonchalant as an accountant emerging from the office at five o'clock. He arched his eyebrows a bit, as if wondering if all police inspectors today were gorgeous chicks like this tall one who had just flashed her badge at him. "He's out of surgery and resting comfortably. Fortunately, only one bullet hit him and it missed his vital organs by a few inches. Really, he's not in bad shape at all. I've seen much worse. He should make a full recovery." To Desirée, he said, "Are you a relative? May I ask your name? Your voice sounds awfully familiar."

"I'm Desirée Dupree."

"On the radio." He nodded to himself as if to say, *So she's the one all this is about.*

"When he's ready to see people," said Christina, "I think Desirée should be the first one. Inspector Cavanaugh's family is flying in from Hawaii as we speak."

"As I understand it," the doctor said to Desirée, "you were in the middle of a shootout not an hour ago. Is that right?"

Desirée swallowed hard. "Yes."

"Then why are you here now?"

"I'm waiting to see about the man who saved my life."

"After such an ordeal, you should be in bed." He looked her up and down. "You're practically vibrating with anxiety."

She offered him the tiniest of shrugs. "Oh, well."

"If you insist on being here, be advised that he won't be awake for several hours. A nurse will escort you up to his room."

"I understand."

The doctor strode off, stretching his arms and hoping that San Francisco's gun-toting maniacs would take the rest of the night off.

"I have to call in," said Christina. She had always prided herself on having the brutal emotional detachment necessary for efficient police work. But now she felt vulnerable, emotional, like the small child she had been once upon a time, weeping on her daddy's knee because of a tiny cut or scrape or just wounded pride. She wanted to be away from Desirée and Monique before she lost control and showed them how human she could truly be.

Christina put a comforting but cool hand on Desirée's shoulder. Desirée pulled her into an embrace so quickly that Christina found herself unable to pry herself loose and, helplessly, burst into passionate tears in the Ragin' Cajun's arms.

After a time, they pulled apart, Christina already dabbing at her eyes and pulling out her cell phone. Desirée turned to Monique, then checked her watch.

"Doc says he'll pull through without much trouble," Monique reminded her. "Got lucky on that one. My med profs are always telling us about how nasty those kinds of injuries are."

"I know he's asleep, but I have to see him. Not sure what I'm gonna say to a man who can't hear me."

"Just say whatever is in your heart."

"If I do that, I'll be in there for ten hours."

"Then wait till the guy walks out of here, marry him and spend the next fifty years telling him what's in your heart," Monique said.

Desirée smirked. "Not a bad idea."

Just then a nurse approached them, her rubber-soled white shoes squeaking on the well-buffed linoleum floor. "Miz Dupree? You may come up to see Mr. Cavanaugh now."

She nodded, her mouth too dry for speech. Perhaps for the first time, she noticed the sterility and austerity of the hospital—the immaculate floors, the gleaming equipment that often was the only thing keeping patients alive, the impersonal politeness of the staff. She wanted to see Harris, regardless of his condition and alertness.

Inside the Intensive Care Unit, he lay asleep in bed, his chest covered in bandages, his face childlike and peaceful. His naturally tan complexion had faded into a pallor resembling the whiteness of the walls surrounding them. Desirée couldn't decide if he looked genuinely happy or simply unconscious and untroubled, temporarily relieved of his earthly burdens. She wanted him to look that way forever, to have him father their children and have them see this serene face every day.

She gazed at his hair, brown and fluffy, soon to need barbering. His shoulders were still broad and muscular, his frame long and lean. Harris Cavanaugh, still a man to be reckoned with.

"You did a good job," she whispered at his bedside, not daring to touch him. There would be plenty of time for that later. "The crazy guy was the electrician. You did what you needed to do. But you took a bullet so I wouldn't have to. That's what

Christina said. You get better and we'll get married, if that's what you want. We'll do whatever you want to do."

Outside the room, Monique urged her to go home and get some sleep. "No, I'll stay here. I'd just as soon climb these walls as the ones at home." Monique reluctantly left and Desirée curled up on a couple of seats in the waiting room, her dreams fitful and perverse, forgotten the moment she awoke to grayish morning sunlight and the noisy busywork of a major metropolitan hospital.

Desirée sat up and ran a hand through her hair. Her bad night had left her muzzy and sweaty. Still, she needed to see Harris again. Maybe he had awakened.

Just then she saw three people coming down the hall. The man was older, tall and gray-haired, wearing a cream-colored linen jacket, walking with the steady gate of someone who refuses to be rushed for any reason. Beside him was a woman, slender and short-haired, chic and fashionable in a Hawaiian dress and sandals, an aging beauty still attractive. The last one was a young woman, hyperkinetic, expecting the rest of the world to keep up with her.

"Let's go find the room," said the older woman, checking room numbers.

"He's in the ICU, Mom," the younger woman said.

"OK, Bonnie, OK. Let's find the I.C.U., then."

The parents went in and Bonnie took a seat at the opposite end of the bench from Desirée. The Cavanaughs, she thought with the smallest of smiles. Bonnie, Harris's M.B.A. sister, trying to cool her heels, fidgety. What would they think if they knew about Harris and this swarthy blonde? Or, rather, what would they think *when* they knew.

When the parents emerged, Bonnie stood up and the man muttered to his wife, "The news reports said he was in a shootout in a radio station. What the hell was he doing there and why weren't there backups? I want to know what was happening, dammit."

"There's time for that," said his wife. "In the meantime, let's be thankful that he's feeling better. His appetite is back. He wanted spicy food. He kept saying he wanted to eat Cajun. I didn't know he went in for Southern cuisine."

Desirée blushed. She got up and walked over to her. "Excuse me, folks, but are you Harris's family?"

"Yes, we are," said the older woman, looking at Desirée as if the swarthy blonde younger woman were some chippie Harris had picked up in a bar and who'd infected him with HIV.

"I'm Desirée Dupree. Harris was probably asking about 'Cajun.' Well, that's me."

"Are you a chef?" she asked.

"No, Cajun is my nickname. Ragin' Cajun, actually. I do a radio show. He was...I was his assignment."

"I see," said the old man with a tone that suggested he had already heard more than he wanted to know. Radio-station shootout? Over a voluptuous blonde with sexy voice, in desperate need of a bath and a good night's sleep? God knew what kind of show she hosted.

Desirée wondered how Harris had gotten along with these people. Probably, they would soon start pressuring the doctor to authorize a transfer to Stanford Medical Center. St. Jude's Hospital was not the kind of place for their boy.

The nurse appeared and said, "Inspector Cavanaugh wishes to see Ms. Dupree next."

"We'll both go in," said Bonnie. Desirée nodded and the two women entered the room.

Harris was watching the door intently as it opened. His face lit up as he saw Desirée, who wasn't sure if he even noticed that his sister, whom he only occasionally saw, was also there.

"Dirty Harry," Desirée said with mock gravity as she nodded at him.

"You're still alive," he murmured, as if her status,

up till that point, had remained a mystery to him. "I've had weird, jumpy images in my head of the KCA hallway and—well, the rest of it is a puzzle."

"You're still alive, too," Desirée said. "You're very lucky."

"I'm a lousy patient. I don't belong here. I wanna go home."

"Which home? Snob Hill or Carmel?" Desirée asked. Bonnie shot her a shocked look, as if wondering just how friendly Harris and the Ragin' Cajun had become.

"I'll let *you* decide."

"As you can see, your sister is here," said Desirée with a theatrical gesture in Bonnie's direction.

Harris nodded. "Heya, Sis."

"So, is the copper going to take an early retirement?" Bonnie asked.

"And do what? Travel like Mom and Dad?"

"Or write your memoirs. Become the next Joseph Wambaugh. Or go get a doctorate degree in philosophy and go teach at some college where you don't get shot."

"Or maybe just keep doing what I've been doing," he said, sounding agitated, as if he had had this conversation with his sister many times by now. "So, I see you've met Desirée. And she looks like hell. She needs to get some sleep. Get security up here to shoo her ass away."

Not smiling at what appeared to be Harris's way of expressing concern, Desirée, whose stomach had been doing somersaults for most of the morning, now felt nauseous. She turned around and marched out of the room. He was right; she looked like hell and needed sleep. Plus a bath and a dose of Pepto-Bismol. She was in no mood for Harris' kidding.

His eyes followed her out of the room. "Nice, huh?"

"Nice voice," said Bonnie. "Nice everything."

Harris cackled. "That's why I love her. She's going to have my baby."

Bonnie's eyes widened. "Is she pregnant?"

"Not yet. But there's plenty of time." He paused. "They just shot me up with morphine before you came by. I want you to know I'm grateful that you care about me." Before she could reply, he added, "I feel so nice and goofy right now." He closed his eyes and went to sleep.

Desirée almost lost it before she made it to the ladies' room. She sprinted past the Cavanaughs and down the hallway, feeling the stomach acid rush up her throat. Bursting into the lavatory, she knelt before the toilet and vomited.

Minutes later, Bonnie entered and walked up to Desirée's stall. The door was open.

Desirée looked up, wiping her mouth. "I didn't mean to be rude."

"Not to worry. Upset stomach?"

The Ragin' Cajun continued wiping her mouth. "Must've been all that vending-machine crap I ate for dinner and breakfast."

"That'll do you in," Bonnie said.

Desirée spat into the toilet. "It nearly did."

"Doctor said the worst is over. He'll be out of here within days."

"He didn't look so bad just now. Don't tell him I puked."

Bonnie smirked. "It'll be our little secret."

"I guess you have a few dozen questions you're dying to ask about the past few months in your brother's life..."

"At least that many. Not that those questions are any of my damn business. But you really *do* need to get some sleep. You look ready to pass out right now. My car is downstairs. I'll drive you home."

"I can get a cab."

"I don't think you heard me. *I have a car.*"

"My home is far away. Out by Mount Davidson."

"So let's get going," Bonnie said.

"Has anyone ever told you that you and Harris are a lot alike?" Desirée asked.

"A few hundred times. He says you're going to have his baby."

"Harris talks a lot of shit."

They both laughed and headed out the door.

...

Jimmy Lee Smith and the KCA shootout became yesterday's news. Desirée did her show as usual. When not at work, she was often at St. Jude's, sitting by Harris's bedside, even when there were other visitors, which was nearly always the case. Harris and she scarcely had a private moment together. When they did, he told her that practically everyone on the San Francisco Police Department, from the chief on down, had come in to say hello. Desirée didn't mind. The visits, and the visitors, tired him easily, and he was on regular doses of painkillers, which always put him to sleep. She was exhausted, too, and started reducing the frequency and duration of her own visits.

They both wanted some downtime. Or so she told herself. Time alone, to forget about what had happened and look forward to what would be.

"Jimmy Lee Smith," Christina Anchor told her, "was a catastrophe waiting to happen. With his upbringing, lack of family support, then coming of age and being shipped off to Vietnam...? It might have been a blessing if he'd been killed in action. Well, he was, in a way. His spirit was a casualty. So he came back home, disoriented and disillusioned, bouncing from city to city in pursuit of some value or goal he would never find. Looking for friendship, he found it with Michael Saburn, another misfit who had some pretty unrealistic expectations in life. So when Michael started fixating on you and you backed off a little bit, that dose of reality tasted awfully sour.

"So what do you do when it becomes clear that

you can't manipulate the universe? Well, if you're as unstable as Michael Saburn, you kill yourself. And if you're Jimmy Lee Smith, you blame Desirée Dupree for Michael's death and resolve to kill her."

"I suppose," said Desirée Dupree, "that it was all inevitable. My rejection of Michael, his suicide and what followed with Jimmy."

Christina nodded. "Inevitable. That it was."

Desirée stuck out her hand. "Anyway, I would like to thank you for the help you gave me during this ordeal. I know I wasn't the most cooperative of assignments."

Christina shook the outstretched hand. "You certainly weren't the worst." She added, "Maybe this isn't any of my business, but I've noticed that you and Harris have developed a significant personal relationship—"

"That's quite an understatement."

"And that's something we're never supposed to do in our profession. Nevertheless, it does happen, even with cop-haters like you. Harris thinks you're good for him, a positive influence."

"He certainly does think that."

"But I wonder if the feeling is mutual. Is a cop who you really want?"

"I guess I'll find out soon enough. He's being discharged soon. Did you know that?"

Christina nodded. "I also know that his professional status is up in the air. When he's well enough, he'll have some decisions to make."

There was no substitute, Desirée concluded, for having a job you liked. So it was with her at KCA. There was no Jimmy Lee Smith around any longer, there were no harassing callers anymore. The hours flew by. Desirée, her concentration as intense as a brain surgeon's, pushed her listeners' buttons and challenged them. She didn't think of evil electricians, cops sitting in the corner or shootouts in the hallway. Each time the on-air conversation got really provocative, it seemed Jay signaled for a break and Desirée sat back to light a Pall Mall. It was not a bad life.

"Desirée Dupree."

She looked up, smiling, and said, "Matt McDonald."

He handed her an unsolicited cup of coffee. "Thought you might like it. Goes well with the smoke."

"You're much too kind." She sipped the coffee, savoring its richness. "So you're back."

Matt nodded. "Indeed I am. I called Kelvin and we talked. He said I could come back. He didn't rag on me or anything. I did have to kiss his ring, though."

"You're lucky that's *all* you had to kiss."

They both laughed. Then Matt said, "I really owe you an apology. The way I showed up at your doorstep and stuck my nose into your private life.

329

That was totally out of line. It was none of my business."

Desirée shrugged. "Already forgotten about, Matt. It was a pretty freaky scene for *all* of us. The cops couldn't catch him...well, you know, enough said."

"I guess I made a fool of myself around you. I'll try minding my manners from now on."

"Hey, I don't mind it that you were attracted to me. Have you met my sister? She doesn't have a boyfriend, you know."

Matt laughed. "Monique? She's way too gorgeous. Totally out of my league."

"Oh, and *I'm* in your league?"

"Shit, Desirée, you know what I mean..."

"That I do, kiddo. That I do."

Just then Jay signalled and Desirée opened up her microphone. "This is the Ragin' Cajun on KCA, Newstalk Nine-eighty, with fifty thousand watts of power. We're heard everywhere from Alaska to

Mexico and everywhere else that someone has Internet access. So just stay tuned...or better yet, call me and you'll be heard. Next up is the national news from Washington, then another hour of open phones."

Matt smiled at the voice he knew so well and loved so much. The news started with the intro music he loved much less. "Another twelve minutes to relax," he noted.

There was a knock on the studio door.

"Mrs. Cavanaugh!" Desirée said, frowning. "Let her in."

Matt opened the door. "Come on in, ma'am. Want some gourmet coffee?"

The woman smiled. "No, thanks. The doctor said it's bad for me."

Matt excused himself. Mrs. Cavanaugh said, "I see you're at work. Is this a bad time?"

"No, it's perfect. We have ten minutes or so

before I have to take calls again. Want a real quick tour of the station?"

"No, I'm pressed for time, too." The woman looked around for the briefest moment. Desirée could only guess at what she thought. Mrs. Cavanaugh no longer looked like a mother under strain because of her son. She now looked like who she was, a trim, pretty older woman of considerable means. Desirée remembered what she had been told of the Cavanaugh family. One of the biggies, here since the Gold Rush days: Hopkins, Huntington, Crocker, Stanford...and Cavanaugh. So here was one of those Cavanaughs, probably a Stanford alumna, standing over Desirée Dupree, the Ragin' Cajun, a blonde, voluptuous radio personality whom her tall, handsome son apparently had every intention of marrying. Desirée stubbed out her cigarette, embarrassed to be seen smoking.

"I just came by to say thanks for being so supportive of Harris. He's going to be released from Saint Jude's soon, so my husband and I are flying back to Maui tomorrow morning. We were in the middle of a vacation when we got the call that he'd been admitted."

"I'm sure it has been quite a difficult week for you."

"No, Desirée, it's you who has had the hard time. Harris told us all about that caller." The woman shook her head. "I can't imagine how you coped."

"It was awful."

Mrs. Cavanaugh reached down and touched Desirée's hand. "Have you and Harris set a wedding date?"

Desirée's eyes bulged. "Excuse me?"

"Oh, I know about the two of you. I was just wondering about the nuptials...if you don't mind my asking."

"Well, ma'am, as they like to say in my business, 'No comment.'"

They laughed.

Jay then signaled to Desirée. Time to go back to work.

Mrs. Cavanaugh left and Desirée did the rest of her shift. At midnight Manny Ramirez came in to relieve her and, as always, she headed down to the parkade.

"Dupree," said the deep male voice she had come to know so well.

"Dirty Harry?" she said, turning around and staring at the leather-jacketed man. He still looked a little unsteady. "Why aren't you in the hospital?"

"Hospitals are boring. Thought I would surprise you. Get in." He gestured to his SFPD car.

"How did you get past security? I'm no longer your assignment."

"I flipped out my tin and told them I had some unfinished business with you. Which is not altogether untrue. Get in."

She shrugged and went towards him. As she

passed him, he grabbed her and kissed her deeply.

Her world spun. She grabbed at him, she wanted to claim all of him for herself. Her hands clutched at his head, then slipped around to grasp his neck. After an eternity, she let him go.

"Well," he managed to say after recovering his composure. "That was worth the wait. Those pitiful little air kisses you gave me at St. Jude's just didn't cut it."

"I didn't want to put on a show in front of your family and associates."

"You could have waited till it was the just the two of us."

"It was never just the two of us. You're too damn popular, Cavanaugh."

"I'll try to be an asshole from now on." Then, "I liked your show tonight."

She shrugged. "It was OK."

"Like hell. It was the best you'd done in a long time. No more monkey on your back. But let me tell you now why I've ambushed you here in the parkade. I want you to know that I'm not trying to pressure you into anything, Desirée. I won't ask you to change and I don't want you to rag on me about what I do for a living."

"You mean because you're a cop?"

"Yeah. And because of a few other things. Where I live and my resources."

"Well, I understand that. You do your thing and I'll do mine."

"No. We do our things together. How do you feel about me?"

"You know I adore you," she said.

"Just 'adore'?"

"I *love* you."

"That's better."

"I was terrified for so long," she said.

"I remember it well."

"I'm starting to put all this behind me now, I guess. Things in my life are starting to settle down and feel right."

"I've asked you before and I'll ask you again. Will you marry me, Desirée?"

She paused, but not because she was unsure she wanted him or because she wanted to make him wait for her answer. She simply wanted to mentally record where they were and what they were doing when this most important question was asked and answered. His unmarked cruiser was not the most romantic of settings. This was not what she had had in mind when, as a little girl, she had dreamed of being proposed to by the man she loved. But here she was, with that very man, in the parkade of where she worked. What the hell.

"There's a matter I need to ask you about," she said.

"Yeah? What's on your mind?"

"It's this: Can we also hire some people to do the stuff we don't want to do?"

"Whatever you want." He leaned over and gave her his longest, most passionate kiss.

She giggled. "Then it's a done deal."

# ABOUT THE AUTHOR

George Onstot, after years of doing boring jobs for low pay, has decided to start publishing the stories many he's written over the years.